BOUND BY THE SCARS WE SHARE
(A TALE OF TWO WOMEN)

About the Author

Vivien Churney is an author, poet and artist, who lives in Liverpool. This is her debut novel.

BOUND BY THE SCARS WE SHARE

(A TALE OF TWO WOMEN)

VIVIEN CHURNEY

Matador
9 Priory Business Park,
Wistow Road, Kibworth Beauchamp,
Leicestershire. LE8 0RX
Tel: 0116 279 2299
Email: books@troubador.co.uk
Web: www.troubador.co.uk/matador
Twitter: @matadorbooks

Grace's story is a work of fiction. All the names, characters, businesses, places, events and incidents are the product of the author's imagination used in a fictitious manner. Any resemblance to actual persons living or dead or actual events is purely coincidental. Zoshia's story is a fictional reconstruction of the author's mother's life. Names, dates, places, events and details have been changed, invented and altered for literary effect. This story should be considered as a work of literary fiction.

ISBN 9781800463400

British Library Cataloguing in Publication Data.
A catalogue record for this book is available from the British Library.

Printed and bound in Great Britain by 4edge Limited
Typeset in 11.5pt Adobe Garamond Pro by Troubador Publishing Ltd, Leicester, UK

Matador is an imprint of Troubador Publishing Ltd

This novel is dedicated to my brave and dear mother, to my father and to all my family and friends who have supported me. I would like to also dedicate this book to those who have struggled for freedom, especially women.

Painting by Vivien Churney

Illustration by Vivien Churney

Belgian Jewish Schoolchildren, prior to WWII

Prologue

Good fortune is a fleeting breeze,
Flighty and fidgety as a child.
It makes you calm and feel at ease,
But its gentle touch soon leaves you behind.
Alas, sorrow clings and holds on tight,
And does not seem to want to depart.
The feeling stays like an endless night,
And remains there like a dagger through your heart.

Vivien Churney

A woman's strength comes from within.
Her intuition is bold and her love is fervent.
The strength of a woman's sadness ripples like her happiness.
Her strength is gentle, yet mighty; ethereal and realistic.
A woman with strength in her soul is a blessing.

Vivien Churney

Zoshia I

It would soon be Shabbos, the Jewish Holy Day. The afternoon sky made subtle shifts in light and shade, darkening slowly as the distant, hazy clouds lazily drifted towards the watery, winter sun. Two days previously, snow had fallen heavily onto the paving stones in the winding streets of Warsaw and its frozen impact metamorphosised into small hillocks of sleet that, in miniature, resembled the icy glacial formations of the Carpathian Mountains which surrounded the Polish city. The Jewish quarter. Footsteps of its inhabitants were rushing hurriedly through the corridors of roads, trying to carve out their lives amongst the sculptures of snow before the setting of the sun. Figures filled the atmosphere with their cloudy breath, as if they too contributed to the life forces in their freezing surroundings. Lining the streets were erect domains, with their first-floor windows open at different angles, to allow the last of the fading sun to penetrate inside and warm the tiny rooms which were inhabited by many of the city's Jewish population.

It was three fifteen in the afternoon. A bearded Jewish man, bent doubled, was walking precariously in slow motion through the deep sludge, carrying a heavy burden which could not be seen. He was a wise man, clutching his books which embodied the learnings of generations. As it was not yet Shabbos, Smule Freedman sat by his small window staring at the cobbled pavements filled with activity – each person was an instrument trying earnestly to play the melody of his life. He could see the vendors; the poor pedlars who would buy and sell whatever they could to make a living. A bit here – a bit there – anything to keep the humanity within their souls in one piece. Each day, the load was carried forward to the next. Smule watched his fellow Jewish people who enlivened the snow-covered streets. Into his view came the learned Rabbis, the grubby beggars; a wooden cart which contained an elderly man who'd had his legs amputated many years ago and was being pulled by his brother; the busy workers, keen to finish and close their shops and the groups of shivering, shawled women brusquely dashing home through the biting weather to prepare Shabbos for their families. He noticed the wealthier men in their fur hats and long coats – well protected from the coldness around them – chatting excitedly under the unlit, blackened lampposts. It was Poland with its slums and markets, businesses and shops, juxtaposing both hope and despair for the future. To Smule, each face revealed a story, a risk, a promise and a destruction. Just at that moment some young, beautiful girls walked slowly past his window, smiling and desiring romance and love from the world; from life, like nightingales singing their sweetest songs just before the darkest hour.

It was Shabbos. The setting sun had faded into shadow and had been devoured by the earth itself. Nightfall had arrived bringing with it the sacred day of rest for all Jewish people. Zara Freedman, Smule's wife, had laid the table according to Jewish tradition for their evening Sabbath meal. The aroma of freshly baked 'Challah' bread purveyed the small sitting room as the wine was opened. Smule, Zara and their beautiful dark-haired, brown-eyed daughter of seven began to partake in the prayer ritual of lighting the Shabbos candles and giving thanks, before eating their lovingly-prepared supper. In the dim candlelight, Zara's saddened face appeared anxious and worried. She felt unable to utter the right words to her beloved little daughter; words which would change everything for her for the rest of her life. Smule sensed his wife's fear and immediately took control. "Hannahla, your mother and I have something very important to tell you. We have been blessed. You are going to have a little sister or brother very soon. It is important that you behave like a good girl and help to take care of the new baby," he gently whispered.

"But I don't want you to love anyone but me," Hannah's childish voice screamed in disbelief. "Please... No... I don't want a brother or sister... I don't" ...as her tantrum became a whimper.

Hannah Freedman was the centre of her parents' world. She was an only child and it was she alone who had received their unconditional love. So it was a devastating shock when her young life was threatened by the imminent arrival of someone who would intrude on their perfect family. At seven years old, sharing was unknown to her. Zara adored little Hannah and doted on her utterly. Tantrums were pacified tactfully and the spirited child always felt that it was she who won any battles with her mother. This time was different however, Hannah was certain that this baby would take her place in her parents' affections.

It was a surprise to Smule and Zara to discover that they would have another child, as they were completely content living in Warsaw with their beloved daughter. Despite the shock, they relished their good fortune and were excited for the forthcoming birth. They had waited a long time before telling Hannah, as they knew what her reaction would be. "I can't believe it, Smule. Another child!" Zara cried to her husband in disbelief. "There will be no more peace for us," she added allowing a smile to appear on her face. Zara was not a physically strong woman and this made her feel some trepidation about the impending birth. "Oh Smule! Do you think I will survive childbirth? I had such a difficult time with Hannah and I pray that it won't happen again."

"Don't worry, Zarala! I will be here to look after you all, you can be sure of that!" he replied protectively, taking her hands lovingly into his own and kissing them.

Smule was a tailor who fashioned garments for both men and women. His stylish designs and quality of fabric cemented his reputation and many people from across Warsaw would come to him to have their clothes made. Short in stature with mocha coloured hair and a determined look in his chestnut eyes, Smule was a popular man with his friends and colleagues. Always direct in his approach, he made others aware that his words were sincere and genuine. A practical man, Smule had learned his trade from his father

Nachum. This helped him to earn a living for his wife and family and to save money for the future. Smule was also a scholar and he loved reading; his home was filled with books comprising of an ample variety of texts. He had a well informed and intellectual understanding of humanity, resulting in his ability to be sensitively aware of people's needs. He cared for others and would often bring complete strangers into his home for his wife to feed. Zara would be exasperated but admired her husband's philanthropic nature. She too was a very caring person, who did not have patience with flippancy or silly behaviour. A strong looking woman in her external appearance hid her rather delicate, inward, physical stamina. With her mahogany, thick hair pulled severely from her face and tied in a chignon at the nape of her neck, Zara projected a stern outward manner but inwardly she was a good natured, compassionate soul. She was a strong support to her husband in his business, by attending to the accounts. Her nimble brain mentally recorded how much each customer had paid. Now she was expecting another child and was extremely nervous about the outcome.

Zoshia Freedman was born on the 1st January 1926. It was an extremely difficult birth which left Zara feeling exhausted and utterly weak. The severe pain of the delivery left a lasting impression on Zara, making it impossible for her to look after her new-born daughter. She could never have imagined the intensity of the agony she had endured; the birth of Hannah had been troublesome but not like this. What had she done to deserve a baby that would cause her so much torment? Unable to take care of Zoshia, Zara hired a local girl, Agata, to help with the burden of her tiny daughter.

Agata Wojcik was eighteen years old and very sweet natured. She loved children and was delighted when Smule and Zara chose her above all the other applicants for the post of nursemaid. Agata relished being in charge of caring for the new-born and made the necessary preparations. When her blue eyes met those of her charge, her heart melted. She felt a sadness for Zara who was trying to cope with the shock of the trauma of her childbirth and yet she enjoyed the time she spent looking after the little one.

So it was a stranger who cared for Zoshia in her early weeks while Zara struggled to bond with the new arrival. How could she love her when all she could think of was the physical suffering that she had caused? The poor infant would often cry, craving the motherly affection that she so desperately needed. But Zara would not heed her daughter's call and pressed her hands to her ears to muffle the shrieks that were so piercing. It was as if Zoshia's lifelong struggle had begun at the moment of her birth, a struggle which would seem to pursue her with a strangled grip. For Hannah, her sister's entrance into her world was unbearable and she was totally consumed by jealousy. Something inside made her hate this intrusion and was determined, at seven years old, to keep control over her parents.

Even though Agata was besotted with Zoshia, she knew that she needed her mother at this early formative time and so she helped Zara tend to her daughter's needs. Zara's initial coldness to her baby gradually disappeared as her maternal instincts took hold. Love and warmth closed the distance between mother and child. She could see lots of herself in Zoshia even then and her heart slowly warmed to those beautiful eyes staring longingly back at her and, as time passed, Zoshia experienced the tenderness and affection which exuded from the kisses and cuddles which the growing baby had yearned for. Zoshia grew into a happy young child who constantly craved physical contact with Zara. But she was always at odds with her sister who would often win the battles in the war for their mother's favour.

In time, these personal issues became secondary to the persecution that Jews had begun to endure from the Polish authorities. Zara and Smule, knew that life as Jews in Poland could no longer be an option. "We have to leave this country, Zara. It is becoming too dangerous to live here. Who knows what may happen to us and the kinder," Smule stated earnestly to his wife, putting his arm around her affectionately and kissing her.

"I know," Zara replied in a trembling voice. "We have to leave for all our sakes. We are being persecuted for just being Jewish. We do not harm anyone, yet we are hated. Why is this happening Smule?" Jews were made to feel separate and inferior, a life which Smule could not bear for his family. He was strong and forceful with a fierce protection of those he loved. His impeccable judgement forced him to make decisions in an instant. Zara, who worshipped her husband, had become weak after Zoshia's birth, and prayed for the persecution to be over. The separateness which they endured seemed impossible and never ending. Although mentally strong, her physical energy was depleted, and the thought of emigrating was overwhelming. She knew in her heart however, that they would have to leave. Europe was the promised land for many Jews and Smule knew that this was the best choice for his family.

Since World War 1, Poland had become an independent state inhabited by many minority populations. However, increasing Polish nationalism made it a hostile place for Jews. A series of pogroms and discriminatory laws were signs of growing antisemitism. Smule had found that his livelihood was threatened because of the growing anti-Jewish policy of the state, where the tax system discriminated against Jewish factory owners and merchants. Smule's tailoring business suffered because buyers and customers boycotted his efforts, as they did all Jewish concerns. It was not just Smule and his family who were leaving; many Jews in Warsaw were also prepared to escape from the persecution in Poland and hoped to commence a new life elsewhere.

Smule made arrangements to leave Warsaw, and emigrate to Antwerp in Belgium; the Jewish population there had been growing slowly for a number of years and Smule believed this would be a safe haven to live as free Jews. Smule's friend, Alek Kaminski, was able to help him acquire the necessary papers for the Freedman family to leave. Smule began to make plans to depart from his sacred homeland, a place which had been tainted for him. He wanted to live a peaceful life and take care of his loved ones. Smule had saved money from his successful tailoring trade and this would enable him to settle elsewhere. Zara respected his plans and knew that she could rely on him to make the right decision. Although she was scared for her family and devastated at leaving her beloved Warsaw, she knew it was the best choice.

The love of her country had been killed by the suppression of the Jews who were treated like second-class citizens.

Smule and his family settled into a tranquil existence in Antwerp. His knowledge of textiles allowed him to establish himself again in the fabric business which would provide for his family. Zara and Smule felt at last that they belonged once more and were part of a community, being no longer made to feel different. They were settled at last and peace seemed to finally embrace them.

Zoshia grew up feeling separate from a young age as her mother poured lavish affection upon her elder daughter to keep her placated. Zara loved her younger child, but did not seem to have time or energy to show her this. Little Zoshia would climb on her mother's knee trying to gain her love and attention. "Mushki," she would cry mournfully. "Can I stay here on your knee and cuddle you?"

Zara would reply in an exasperated tone, "I'm busy now. Can't you see that my Hannah needs me? Later! Now please stop whining!" Hannah ruled the household and Zoshia quickly learned to get used to it and instead found comfort in her toys, which replaced human affection for her.

As time passed, Zoshia emerged as a clever and talented child who excelled at school; placed in a class with older children, Zoshia became mature beyond her years. She would rush home to tell her mother about her academic achievements in the vain hope of getting some recognition, but continued to be tortured by feelings of rejection when her mother seemingly ignored her. On the odd occasion Zara would praise her calling her a clever girl and Zoshia would beam with pride and happiness in these moments of approval – her blue eyes would sparkle with glee, as if her whole being would explode. But this affection would never last for long as she was constantly overlooked in favour of Hannah.

Hannah grew into a very beautiful teenage girl, with her dark complexion and her coal-black hair, but she still held resentment for her younger sister who she thought had taken away everything from her. Clever and talented, her sister seemed to make her parents proud in ways that she never could. Hannah could not discard her powerful envy even though deep down she did love the little girl who played the piano so beautifully. But unable to master the instrument herself, Zoshia's sister felt inferior and incapable in comparison. In order to compensate, she lured her parents' attention whenever they appeared to focus their interest upon her sister. Zoshia soon realised the extent of control Hannah had over them.

Although Zoshia continued avidly with her studies and played the piano, which comforted her, she still felt isolated. The more lonely she felt and the more her inferiority plagued her, the greater her success became in all her achievements. She developed into a gifted piano player who had been taught well by her German teacher, Gunther Bohm.

Gunther was a very tall, pencil-thin man with an unruly mop of blonde hair which sometimes seemed unkempt. He was a perfectionist and instilled this into Zoshia, who dared not make a mistake in case he rapped her tiny fingers with his baton. While she was playing, he would wave this instrument in the air in time to the music and only lowered it when his ears felt insulted by the notes that she played incorrectly from time to time. Zoshia knew that the only way to escape her teacher's wrath was to practise until she knew each piece perfectly. This was sometimes very difficult for her, as Hannah would deliberately scream at the top of her voice so that Zoshia could not stand the noise a moment longer. Frequently, Zara would ask Zoshia to refrain from playing in order to placate Hannah. Zoshia's mother was inwardly extremely proud of her daughter's talent but she had to appease her older child or life would have been totally unbearable. So to avoid such confrontation, Zoshia would sometimes play the notes in silence with her fingertips hovering over the keys and hear the music in her head.

Despite Zoshia's loneliness at home, she had two close school friends, Regene and Anna, who supported her emotionally and went some way towards giving her the comfort she needed. Zoshia adored them. Regine was very petite with copper-coloured hair in a mass of curls, and her heart shaped face was covered in freckles. She had a cheerful toothy smile which made her very endearing. Regine loved to play with Zoshia, and her friend sensed her love and admiration. They both enjoyed their friendship with Anna, a large round child, with thick black curls which formed a halo around her head. Her large brown eyes glistened with excitement when they sang together and danced holding hands.

Like her father, Zoshia was unable to bear injustice. Despite her detached relationship with her mother, she often spent some time with Smule when Hannah was with Zara. Her father would speak to her about his life in Poland and how the Jews were unfairly treated. He informed Zoshia about her relatives who still lived in Warsaw, who were suffering harsh discrimination and had found it difficult to leave. Zoshia was horrified. She could not stand cruelty in any form and was always helping others in school who may have been bullied or felt that they were lonely. Zoshia would always offer them friendship and somehow this would compensate for her feelings of rejection by her own mother. The older she grew, the more her sense of morality gained in stature. Zara would often rebuke her for getting involved in her friends' problems or difficulties, but Zoshia always felt that she had accomplished something worthwhile when she helped others.

As the Freedman family went about their daily routine, a darkness grew unnervingly within the community and there was no escape from uttering the name Adolph Hitler, whose armies were marching into the surrounding countries. Germany was at war. Everyone was frightened, but the Jewish people of Antwerp were petrified. Antisemitism was flourishing once again and threatened the Freedman family, like all other Jewish families who sensed that their days of freedom and peace would soon be crushed by war. The cruel insect of persecution had followed them. "Was it a crime to be Jewish?" Smule would ask his wife, in desperation. Zara could not bear to answer.

With Germany at war, Zoshia felt an overwhelming sense of doom. She knew this life she had grown to love would be fractured beyond repair. It was this dread that compelled her to gather all her Jewish school friends for a photograph. It might be the last time they would all be together like this. Smule made the arrangements with Zoshia's schoolteacher.

When the photograph was developed, Zoshia knew she would treasure it forever, despite the uncertainties of an unknown future. It would remind her that somewhere in her life, there had been fondness, tenderness, warmth and compassion. Her childhood innocence was encapsulated in this tiny memento.

Grace 2

Lyme Regis, once a large port, proudly boasted a breakwater and harbour that nestled by the sea on the West Dorset coast. The rugged surrounding landscape was reminiscent of a world dominated by dinosaurs and large reptiles who once ruled the earth. Here was a picturesque scene of beauty as the froth laden waves would nod gently onto the sandy shoreline. This deceptive landscape could often change at any moment when Lyme Regis was exposed to a south-westerly gale. The menacing wind would howl like a wildcat and, even though invisible, it could create immense damage to the delicate, pretty cottages which framed the steep, narrow streets that rushed directly down to the massive stone clad jetty named The Cobb, which majestically guarded the harbour. Lyme Regis, gracefully described as 'The Pearl of Dorset' was framed by the dark, threatening cliffs that boldly ruled the charming landscape with an iron grip. The clouds that crowned the mountains would create a sullen shadow displacing the sun's rays and replacing them with gloom.

Edward Brookfield was born in this area with its abundance of fossils. He was the seventh child from an authoritarian family and his father, Herbert, was a forceful disciplinarian and was uncompromising in his beliefs. His austere attitude contrasted with his engaging, amiable wife Beatrice, who Herbert treasured and cherished. The couple loved their children but their father insisted upon strictness as he believed that this would help them develop into worthy adults. Secretly, Beatrice would disobey her husband and give her children the affection and humour which their father lacked. Sometimes, Beatrice would cry herself to sleep at night because of what she believed to be the cruelty that her husband inflicted on their precious ones. Her anxiety escalated, and one Wednesday morning in 1913, when Edward was just four years old, Beatrice put on her hat, scarf and coat, walked out of the house and was never seen or heard of again. Edward, as the youngest child, adored his mother and was utterly crushed and horrified when he realised that she was never to return. A gentle boy, Edward's hurt turned to suppressed anger. He grew up feeling intense shame at Beatrice's behaviour. This consequently caused him to develop a hatred towards the opposite sex.

As a young man he found it difficult to make friendships with women. He saw them as 'the enemy'; believing that all females had loose morals and that he would never be ensnared by one. He thought that his mother had tricked his father and himself by making a pretence of sincerity and love. Edward imagined that Beatrice had betrayed them all and had left them for her lover.

In church, which he attended every Sunday, he found himself attracted to a local girl, Jean Loftus, who would sit with her head lowered and her hands clasped on her knees. Could he allow himself to develop feelings for this plain unassuming person? Edward wasn't sure and felt very nervous at approaching the situation. As a young boy, he had seriously injured his arm and as a result it hung limply by his side. This made him inwardly doubt his manhood and consequently he hid his insecurities by behaving like his father in a strict and disciplined manner. His attitude to life was dictated by Beatrice's behaviour. Despite this, he eventually married Jean who was a meek and timid woman. She had been brought up to speak only when spoken to by her clergyman father. Jean knew nothing about life as she was overprotected by her parents, who believed that they were ensuring she would come to no harm.

Edward would visit church each Sunday and sit near to the Loftus family. After many months, a friendship ensued, and a marriage was arranged. Jean was a woman who firmly believed that it was a man's world and all her life she had wished to become a dutiful wife just like her mother. Adoring her husband, she lived to make him happy, thinking absolutely nothing of her own needs. Edward loved Jean's demeanour and temperament. She never really looked into his eyes and usually walked with her head bowed in subservience. The match was approved by her parents – Edward was an accountant and was financially stable enough to provide for their daughter.

It was Easter Sunday 1932 (one year after Edward and Jean's wedding), at 11am, when Grace Brookfield was born. It was an easy delivery and Jean stoically endured the discomfort. The church bells rang loudly at the exact time of the birth but it seemed as if Grace's cries were even louder. Jean would say to Grace, years later as a young adult, that her cries on that day foreshadowed the cries she would be bellowing throughout her life.

Being the first-born child, Grace often wished she had been born a boy as this is what her father told her he had longed for. Edward's animosity towards the female sex had an enormous effect on his daughter. When Jean gave birth to a son, four years later, it was a total shock but an utter delight for the proud parents. He was worshipped and doted on, beyond anything that little Grace could imagine. Even at the tender age of four, she could see how much adoration her little brother George received. From the moment he was born, Grace felt forever his inferior.

While growing up, she fervently tried to hide the girlishness which she hated in herself and became a tomboy, all in the hope that this would guarantee the love and attention which George received, just because of his sex. She would tuck her hair away haphazardly and love to run freely in the mud and jump in puddles in their large garden. She was, in fact, much tougher and stronger than George, who was more reserved and sullen. Grace loved to push him over playfully so that he would become dirty and unkempt, just like her, hoping that he would get into trouble. This would result in him crying and running to his mother. Jean would always blame Grace and she would often receive a merciless beating by Edward as punishment. Grace would scream in pain and run into the garden, rolling in the soil and greenery to help admonish the stings on her skin. A child of nature, Grace relished the sensation of the soft grass on her body. Somehow, it gave her inner comfort. She often appeared, despite her beauty, dishevelled and scruffy, but she didn't care how she looked. Even as a child, her beauty was mesmerising. Her steel blue eyes and flaxen curls made her look like a china doll, but her external appearance concealed inner cracks. She felt a misery inside her which she constantly hid, in case her father shouted at her. Her looks attracted attention and adoration from family relatives and friends, but never from her parents.

Edward was determined that his daughter would not grow up like his mother. He would continue to subdue and control her with his coldness. He criticised her continually during mealtimes for not holding her spoon properly or slouching at the table. She was not allowed to speak and was forced to eat in silence. Grace became terrified before each meal and could not bear to eat. Keeping her food in her mouth and refusing to swallow gave her a feeling of control. Jean was determinedly patient and would gently press the morsels held in her cheeks until there was no choice but to swallow. The little child could not understand why her parents, particularly her father showed no warmth. She wondered why he did not love her. Edward believed that it was his duty to prepare his daughter to become exactly like his wife, obedient. When he looked at Grace, he could not bear her angelic allure which made people comment. Whenever her beauty was praised, he would always mention his son. Jean was silent and stoic, with a deference to her husband which made her ignore his emotional cruelty to their daughter. As a result, Grace became sad and sullen, causing her to misbehave at school, where she was continually reprimanded.

Ballet was Grace's passion. It was during her ballet lessons that she felt permitted to become the female part of herself. Attending classes with her ballet teacher, Mrs Ellison, Grace adored the warm-up exercises and the different movements but best of all she became alive when she had to perform a dance routine as the final part of the session. Lillian Ellison had once been a principal dancer with a London ballet company. Unfortunately, she had sustained an injury to her fibula which had only partially healed and was therefore forced to abandon her promising ballet career. She was devastated for many months until she decided to move to Lyme Regis, where she lived with an old schoolfriend, who encouraged her to become a dance teacher. Lillian's hair had turned grey and she wore it hanging freely despite encouraging her pupils to wear the traditional hair style of a ballerina. Her face displayed a permanent smile, reflecting her love of dancing. When she noticed Grace performing with such poise and refinement for a six year old, she realised very quickly that this star pupil was extremely talented and so pushed her much further than the other young dancers. Mrs Ellison encouraged her to participate in various local performances as well as entering her for graded ballet examinations. At six years old, Grace showed much promise and her talent was clearly evident. She excelled with her innate flair and technical prowess which earned her numerous awards. Frequently she would show her parents each certificate or a medal she had won, in a vain attempt to receive their praise and pride. "We pay for your lessons, Grace, so you should be excelling," Edward would repeatedly reply in an arrogant and condescending manner. "You don't, however, seem to be achieving very highly at school, now do you? You are poor at your sums and you are behind with your tables. This is not good enough. Try harder." Grace would run out into the garden and weep violently until she felt completely empty. Her tiny fingers would dig into the cool grass, as she gripped the blades for the solace it gave her.

Alongside dancing, drawing and painting allowed Grace to express her deepest feelings. Having a vivid imagination, she invented all kinds of unusual creatures to sketch which she believed existed in other worlds. "I will never understand how you could possibly draw such horrible monsters," Jean reprimanded. Grace did not reply, because she felt her mother knew best. She also loved to copy the free flowing grace and beauty of the dancers in her ballet books. This her mother approved of and admired her little girl's talent, although she never voiced it. Edward was uninterested in Grace's drawings and she was unable to consult him about anything to do with her pictures. Even though she was barely seven years old, she was discerning and understood the wrath of her father and the delirious rages which might occur should she endeavour to do something wrong in his eyes. The balance between harmony and discord was precarious and Grace lived part of her childhood in fear and the other half enjoying her talents and playing in the outdoors, inspecting ladybirds and making daisy chains.

Britain and France declared war on Germany when Grace was seven years old, following Adolph Hilter's invasion of Poland. When Neville Chamberlain announced that Britain was at war with Germany, everyone in the Brookfield family was devastated. Whole communities were shocked in disbelief. Another war! Could this really be true? They all knew that life would never be the same again. Prior to the announcement, Edward had been offered a lucrative position as an accountant in Harpenden, Hertfordshire. Given that his new position offered much more money than they had been used to, Edward and Jean felt this was too good an opportunity to pass up despite the risk of possible bombings. The Brookfields decided that Grace would stay with Edward's brother and his wife in Lyme Regis for her own safety and they would take George with them, unable to be separated from their precious child.

Uncle Peter and Aunt Margaret lavished affection upon their niece as they had been unable to have children themselves. Peter Brookfield had also been brought up strictly by Herbert and often had to supress his excitable feelings, due to his extreme fear of his father's wrath. He was a tall, thin man with carrot-coloured wispy hair and his poor eyesight caused him to wear brown round-lensed metal glasses. His thin lips displayed a wry smile and his watery grey eyes twinkled whenever Grace was around. Unlike his brother, Peter was not academic. He loved nature and always wanted to be a farmer. Margaret Brookfield was a buxom wholesome woman who yearned desperately for a child. Her rosy cheeks prominent and round, framed a large smile which seemed to envelope her whole face. With her dark-brown, thick hair tied into a bun, on top of her head, Margaret appeared as a friendly, jovial woman who adored her niece. She was delighted to have sole charge of this tiny little girl, even for a short while. This was a perfect gift, a young child who seemed to adore them.

Peter and Margaret lived on a small farm and they worked hard on a daily basis to maintain their income which their smallholding provided. They had several cows and during the early hours would ensure that the milk was ready for collection. The chickens cackled each day to be fed. Grace loved to watch Narla, their sheep dog, barking at them from the farmhouse. She also loved to help pick the strawberries, some of which she took and ate in secret. There was a contentment when she visited the farm as she delighted in the natural world. This atmosphere filled the vacuum of loneliness which had been created by frequent condemnation and fault-finding from her parents. She had always dreamed of being able to live there and to help take care of the animals.

Grace was very thrilled to be allowed to stay on the farm, yet she was a bit apprehensive about her parents going away. Her excitement was compounded by the fact that the constant criticism would be abated. She worshipped her aunt and uncle, particularly Uncle Peter who would swing her round and round until she felt dizzy – she loved the exhilaration.

"Now Grace, you must behave yourself while we are away. There is a war on, and we all must be very brave. Your brother is still very young, so we have to take him. Your uncle and aunt will take care of you. Please do as they say."

Edward spoke this in a low, unemotional voice, as might be spoken to a pet dog. "We know that you can be a good girl if you try. So, listen to your father and obey Uncle Peter and Aunt Margaret," he added pointing his finger directly between her eyes. Grace took hold of her aunt's hand, as her mother, father and her brother walked down the path to their car. Jean fashioned a wave and promptly patted her son on the head.

As her parents departed, she waved goodbye while pirouetting around Uncle Peter's front room, as they disappeared into the distance.

Zoshia 3

At fourteen years old, Zoshia had grown into a beautiful, mature, young woman, with gold hair, a pale, creamy skin and mournful, blue eyes, which were captivating and compelling. She continued to play the piano and Gunther was extremely proud of his protégé. He recognised her talent and believed that she played better than most adults he had taught. Zoshia displayed a sensitivity for music which he adored. He knew in his heart that if she carried on with this vocation, that one day she would be able to play in the most glorious concert halls throughout the world and he was delighted that it was he alone who had nurtured her genius and flair from a very young age. Zoshia loved her piano and adored Gunther, who she recognised as a gifted musician. It was with great sadness however, that Gunther told his pupil that he would have to stop teaching her. Zoshia was utterly devastated. He had taught her so much about music but also helped her master the German language. He apologised profusely but explained that circumstances beyond his control prevented him from continuing. He left, knowing that he would never see his musical disciple again. He left to join the German army.

In 1940 German soldiers marched menacingly into Antwerp with a murderous spring in their steps, carrying orders to destroy and ultimately exterminate the Jews living there. As the Nazi invaders paraded along the road, they were accompanied by huge metallic monsters, slowly and determinedly entering the streets; a pack of voracious lions ready to destroy their prey, with the leader of the pack sitting proudly astride his tank, enjoying the fear that he was creating amongst the petrified Jewish and Gentile population who had been conquered by Hitler's army. Fearing the Germans, many Jewish families living in the city fled to other parts of Belgium in the hope of escaping torture and death. The military government passed a series of anti-Jewish laws which enabled them to seize Jewish-owned businesses and to railroad all Jews out of civil service positions. The Antwerp pogrom followed and two synagogues, the centre of Jewish life, were callously burned down. As time passed, Jews were forced to register in a special 'Juden register' so that the government could identify all Jews living in Antwerp. They were forbidden to leave their homes from evening till morning and were not permitted to enter pubic parks. The German authorities deported a large number of Jews to rural areas in the Belgian province of Limbourg. Eventually all Jews were compelled to display the yellow badge. Mass arrests of Jews were initiated throughout Belgium. A transit camp was opened at Mechelen and from there, the human fodder was deported to the Nazi concentration camps of Central and Eastern Europe. This was the living hell which ruthlessly and heartlessly stole the precious souls of these innocent victims. The Freedman family were fortunate to have had Belgian citizenship and were able to remain hidden for a while.

It was terrifying for Zoshia and Hannah to hear the thundering footsteps of the German butchers in uniform and the agonising screams emanating from outside. It petrified them to look through the window and see men and women being brutally beaten and thrashed. Jews were being ordered not to walk on the pavement but in the gutters. Houses were broken into and shop fronts were smashed violently. Glass was flying through the air like snowstorms in the bitter cold and painted on the fronts of Jewish houses were the words 'Juden' and 'Schwein'. Huge stars of David were sprayed randomly across the doors. Evil continually sprang and took its insidious hold.

On one occasion when Zoshia dared to peer through the net curtains, she saw two young Jewish children walking in a huddled fashion close to their parents who were bent over, as if they were trying to be inconspicuous. How their yellow stars glared brightly! Two German soldiers tore the children, by their hair, away from their parents and hurled them into a waiting van. When the shocked people of the gathering crowd pathetically pleaded with the soldiers for the lives of the parents, they were both shot instantly. The gunshot sent a chill through Zoshia. Choking on her vomit, Zoshia ran to the bathroom. When she returned to the living room she looked desperate and shaken "Why Papa? How could human beings do such a thing?" she asked Smule with tears stinging her face.

"They are not human. They are monsters. Tonight has shown that. We must be extremely careful," he replied, clearing his throat so that he did not let Zoshia sense his own fear. Their terror was far beyond anything they could have imagined and the Freedmans became accustomed to the sounds of their own heartbeats thumping and pounding as if they would explode. They had not yet been discovered as being Jews because Smule had the foresight to close his shop before the impending arrival of the invaders.

The family continued to hide in their apartment, except for Zoshia who would go out bravely to purchase essential provisions. With her blonde hair, blue eyes and pale skin, Zoshia was able to create the illusion that she was a Gentile. She wore a large cross around her neck, which helped her to take on this character and project the required image. She felt guilty at this outward betrayal of her faith, but she kept the true sense of herself within her heart. Zoshia knew that venturing out every day was a gamble but this was her contribution to help her family survive.

The first time she risked going out alone, the anxiety and terror that Zoshia felt as she walked through the streets of Antwerp was all consuming. It was as if she could feel everyone looking at her saying, 'THERE IS A JEW.' Zoshia took control of herself as her inner voice directed her to… "be strong"… "don't look down"… "look straight ahead and be confident." Despite this, she heard her fearful voice telling her… "they know"… "they are going to shoot me." Zoshia could see wild flames and clouds of black, bellowing smoke emanating from the apartment blocks where fellow Jews had lived. She could see and hear the fearsome sounds of the large jackboots ferociously kicking Jewish men and when they fell, there was the reverberation of several shots; the certainty of a job done properly. There seemed to be endless vans being driven back and forth and soldiers randomly collecting people to be ruthlessly thrown into them. A refusal or a plea would mean instant death. Bodies were dragged violently and mercilessly from their homes like pieces of blood-soaked raw meat ready to be taken to the abattoir. Zoshia had to bite her lip to prevent herself from hitting out at these vicious and savage sadists. The clouds of human grief enveloped her as she presented an outward show of nonchalance. Just before she went into the shop, Zoshia nervously walked past a German soldier who was fighting with a woman who was holding steadfastly onto her little boy. Screams and shrieks resounded through the atmosphere as the little boy, whose arm had been ripped off by the soldier while he dragged him from his mother, was callously thrown into the van; his limb was left on the ground and his beaten mother accompanied her son in the van with blood gushing and splashing him. Zoshia ran urgently into the shop having quickly swallowed and stopped herself being sick, so that no one could see her distress. She could not reveal what she had seen to her parents, as it would devastate them to know that their daughter had been exposed to such horror. "I have to keep going," she thought to herself. "I am strong and Papa knows this. I have to help; I have to."

Smule and Zoshia were part of the Comité de Défense des Juifs which was a co-ordinated resistance movement that helped to organise food, refuge and hiding to support other Jews who were desperate. All the members came from areas of political and religious diversity. Some of them were from non-Jewish Belgian families who managed to hide, and support Jews who might be deported. Smule would often sneak out at night, if he was needed, to help anyone. If he was caught, he had his false papers. But the threat had not yet materialised and he hadn't been noticed. Zoshia would often help by taking children to hide with non-Jewish Belgian families and in Catholic convents.

The fateful day came. Their worst fears were now a reality: Jewish registration records arrived through the post and Smule knew at once that they had reached the point where they would have to go into protected hiding. All Jews had been sent these documents. So far, they had managed to remain in their home without having been discovered. But this was it! Why had they been sent papers to sign? Had someone told the authorities that there were Jews living at this address? This was risky now, Smule thought to himself. We will have to do something urgently. Hannah kept insisting that it would be illegal not to sign and fervently tried to persuade him to do so.

"Papa, you can't just leave it! It is illegal not to sign. You will be found out and we will be caught! You must sign, Papa! Everyone else has."

Smule replied adamantly, "Rip up all papers! We will not sign anything; this paper is our death warrant, and our signatures will mark us. If we sign we are doomed. They will trace us. Absolutely not!" It did not worry Smule that he would be different; he instinctively knew the right course of action to take in a crisis. As a young woman, Hannah was always determined to get her own way, but this time she had failed. Smule was steadfast in his resolve.

Zara agreed with her husband that they should act quickly. Through his contacts in the Belgian Resistance, Smule obtained alternative false identities. They moved with speed to different premises: some attic rooms owned by a gentile neighbour, Madame de Smett. In the past, Smule had supplied her with material and had tailored suits for her. They had become friends. Madame de Smett was an honest, sincere woman who was helping the Jews in their plight and offered the Freedmans a lifeline. She lived with her husband, Monsieur Paul de Smett, who was a banker. They had one daughter Marie who they had adopted. Each day when Marie left for school with her father, his wife would take provisions up to the attic for the Freedmans, who relished everything they were given. They even began to look forward to the dried peas from which they made 'coffee'. Marie was not to know in case she told her friends. The tiny attic, though a safe haven for the moment, seemed to crush their bodies as they stooped to walk around. A makeshift toilet was minuscule, in a man-made separate room, which allowed them a hint of modesty. Each day Madame de Smett would take their ablutions and dispose of them. Their beds were four flat mattresses with horsehair blankets. In the corner of the room was a sink with running cold water. Washing in cold water was something they would have to get used to. A primus stove enabled them to heat enough water to drink and made it possible for them to cook some food. Belgian citizens were heavily restricted in terms of the amount of food they could purchase – each person would only be afforded 225 grams of bread a day and 250 grams of butter, 1kg of meat and 15kg of potatoes each month. This was all Zoshia was able to obtain and this had to be shared between the four of them.

“How long are we going to have to stay in?“ Hannah implored her father. Zoshia is able to go outside. It’s not fair! We are cooped up here, while she is out!” Smule loved his daughter and had to find ways to pacify her. “It won’t be long now, my Hannah. Zoshia brings us food, doesn’t she?” Hannah did not reply.

This way of life had a profound effect on Zoshia who had to live in a world of horror, always wondering when they would be discovered and deported to a concentration camp with thousands of others. It was still essential for her to obtain food as this would supplement the provisions which Madame de Smett brought. Zoshia insisted on this. She knew her own inner strength. Every day she would have to walk past the German soldiers who would whistle and leer at her, making her skin crawl. Her apparent Arian beauty attracted a soldier on her way home one afternoon. “Ah, meine schönheit,” she could hear him call, after a menacing whistle and an evil snigger. She used every strength of her being to ignore him and walk at a steady, self-controlled pace. Faster! Her legs moved quicker! She ran. Zoshia could hear her heart beating so strongly and so swiftly, that it was as if some interior drumstick was hitting her chest. Her body was soaked and drenched, dripping with sweat as she tried to run as fast as she could. Suddenly she felt a strong arm grabbing her roughly. She stood rigid and was now completely powerless to do anything as the monster held her with a forceful, fierce, vice-like grip and put his strong, muscular arm tightly around her waist. She felt utterly nauseous and in an instant, she vomited voraciously with fear and anxiety over his immense black jackboots. She felt as though she would never stop. It was as if she was subjecting him to the wrath of the entire Jewish people. The shock of this promptly and miraculously stopped him from pursuing her further and she managed to escape his clutches.

Zoshia intended to keep this incident to herself, but she could not sustain the silence. She had to share the experience even though it was heart-breaking to do so. "I feared for my life, Papa," Zoshia told Smule, weeping uncontrollably.

"My poor, babala," he replied, not daring to show her how he really felt. "We must leave as soon as possible," he stated, with a determination in his voice.

"But where can we go?" Zara whimpered. "We can't move again, can we?" She was petrified, but tried not to let them see.

"We cannot stay here," Smule responded knowing that he would have to contact his friends in the resistance movement to arrange a plan. Madame De Smet would ensure that Smule's contacts would be made aware of the situation.

Once again new papers, and further false identities were arranged as the Freedmans planned their escape to Central France. They had to evade the persecution from the Nazis which would almost certainly result in transportation to a death camp or immediate annihilation.

They packed minimally for their trip to Limoges and during the darkness of the night they were huddled into a van which was filled with hay. There was a false bottom under which Smule and his family were hidden. This was an extremely dangerous expedition and Alan Janseens, the driver, was risking his own life to take the charges to safety. As he was part of the underground movement in Antwerp, he was experienced at helping Jews to escape. It was a long arduous journey. When he approached an overgrown area of the French countryside, he stopped and allowed his passengers to attend to their personal needs. Zoshia was stoic in her approach to this situation but poor Hannah begged her father to allow her to sit in the front with the driver. Alan told her severely, that she should obey her father and remain hidden. It was possible that they would be discovered, and that the outcome would be far worse than hiding under some hay. Each time they stopped, the situation was the same.

It seemed like they had been travelling continually for such a lengthy period of time and everyone eventually fell asleep. Suddenly, the van shuddered and stopped. They could hear sharp voices. Alan was asked, by German soldiers, to show his papers. Terrified, Zoshia held her sister's leg tightly. Smule grasped Zara's hand firmly. Had he brought his family into this danger only to end up dead? Was he foolish to have done this? The soldiers inspected the van and prodded the hay aggressively with their rifles. The noise could be heard from the Freedman's hiding place but they remained completely still, barely daring to take breath. As they did not find anything, the soldiers allowed Alan to continue with his journey. The family were petrified and it took every ounce of their energy to cope with the anxiety and carry on. Eventually, after an extremely long and onerous journey, they arrived at a farm in Limoges, where they were led by a French Resistance worker, to where they would be staying.

Their refuge was a large barn. Many of their needs were catered for by Monsieur Duchamps, a member of the French Resistance Movement who aided Jews to hide from the deadly enemy. His wife, Lorraine, helped Zara by providing them all with comfortable bedding and curtains, to divide up the space for some privacy. To the rear of the barn, there was a toilet and a rusty wash basin. This was a delight. Every small gift was a luxury.

Everyone settled into their accommodation and endeavoured to make the best of their life. They did not have much reading material to pass the time away; just a few books which Zoshia and her father had managed to pack. Frequently, they would sing quietly together and each one of them took turns to tell stories. Zoshia would often look at her picture of her friends and wondered whether they were safe. She liked to sit and imagine what it would be like in the future when the war would be over, and they could play once more. But Zoshia knew, that those childhood days were gone forever. She was no longer a child but an adult, who had to endure this tortuous life like a caged animal. Worried for her parents, she would often try to make them laugh with imagined jokes or jocular antics. Hannah was extremely unhappy, and no amount of cajoling could change her miserable persona. She felt deprived of her life as resentment built up inside her about her captivity. Hannah was allergic to hay and sneezed continually. Unable to bear it, she constantly moaned and groaned to everyone. She was not alone in her suffering. Zoshia also experienced the utter misery of being constantly bitten by mosquitos. Being forced to remain indoors, especially in the heat was utterly unbearable for them.

They were prevented from going out for fear of being discovered by German soldiers, who often did spot checks on the farms. One afternoon, the sounds of overhead aircraft could be heard like invading aliens zooming high and low. Zoshia pressed her ears tightly to drown out the sound and cried, "I can't stand this, Papa! How long will this go on for? I am bitten. I itch. I can't stand it!" Hannah also complained bitterly and begged, "Please can we go outside for a while?"

Smule at once took control of the situation and reprimanded them. "Don't you see that we are here for our very survival? We cannot take the risk of being discovered. We will be sent to the gas chambers which I can assure you is a lot worse than a few bites or some sneezing. You will have to make the best of it. We have shelter, food and drink. No more moaning!" He knew how hard it was for his precious daughters but did not want to weaken because of their suffering. He had to be strong for all of them, including Zara, who was often quiet and withdrawn.

Unusually, it was Zoshia who eventually disobeyed her father. One morning, she felt compelled to feel what was outside. Slowly and silently, she crept out when the family were still sleeping. She carefully opened the door of the barn and cautiously closed it behind her. At last! Zoshia felt the warm air on her cheeks and smelt the sweet aroma of the luxurious grassland which surrounded her. The sky was a blanket of blue, enveloping her whole being, and encouraging a calmness which in turn created a sense of freedom. Its immensity combined with the energy emitted from the swaying trees, gave her a feeling that she hadn't experienced for some time. She felt at once a sense of herself as part of the universe. The silence was deafening as she ran as fast as she could, while feeling the grassland under her feet. She ran as if she would never stop until the sound of an aeroplane flying above her, brought her back to reality. She immediately fell on the ground, hidden by the tall blades of grass. The plane seemed to hover in mid-air. Zoshia didn't dare to breathe. As peace reappeared, she lifted her eyes towards heaven. The German pilots, who might have spotted her from the plane and landed, continued to fly into the distance. When Zoshia realised this, she crawled like a small caterpillar back to the barn. She was much too frightened to stand up. Zoshia was greeted by Madame Duchamps, who held her close and restored her to Smule and Sarah, who were so anxious that they could not reprimand her. They understood why she had gone out and she had learned her lesson the hard way.

For months after this event, Zoshia was pensive and did not communicate with her family. The feeling of helplessness which she felt was more than she could bear. Smule had told her that many young people in France were appalled by the occupation of the Nazi government and had formed a resistance movement to help sabotage the control of the German forces. Zoshia desperately wanted to do something to assist in the downfall of the evil perpetrators of the destruction of the Jews and told her father of her intention.

"Where have you got these foolish ideas from, Zoshela? You cannot expect me to allow you to risk your life," Smule told her, in a voice which faltered. He knew how brave his young daughter had become. Zara stated that if Zoshia could help the French Resistance to take young children to the Swiss border, she might be allowed to stay in the country and would therefore be saved.

"Oh yes… please Papa!! I want to help. Please I have to do something," Zoshia implored her father. He knew the resolve which Zoshia felt in her heart and that this was what she had to do. Despite his reservations and fear of the consequences of her being caught, he eventually relented.

The French Resistance movement was affiliated to a wide network of people who helped to transfer Jewish children across a large terrain of land which separated France from Switzerland. They were helped by a group of Swiss men and women who were prepared to defy the Nazis by using knowledge of the tracks and cliff entrances to the huge forest which was unused by the authorities.

Zoshia was questioned by those in charge of the movement. She was accepted and trained for six weeks on all aspects of physical and mental requirements which would be needed during her journeys through the woods. Of course she was terrified, but knew that this was the right pathway for her to take. She also felt valued as being part of something so urgent and important.

At last she was assigned to a young man, Pierre Moulin, who would be her guide in taking eight young children through the rough terrain of the Risoux forest during the icy coldness of winter. This would be a petrifying experience for her but Zoshia knew that the most important thing was that she should protect the children, who were just ten years old, and a couple of them a bit younger. Pierre would concentrate on their route, to avoid the German soldiers, who would, in an instant, shoot to kill anyone they saw.

Zoshia had been told by her parents to try and remain in Switzerland once she had transferred the children there. She hoped this would be the case but did not dare to think about it. Although she desperately desired this haven, the thought of securing her own safety while the lives of her family were still in peril was unbearable.

Having arrived by train at Thonon-Les-Bains Station and all with false papers, they rushed to the nearby snow-covered forest which would help to shield them from any soldiers. It was dim, cold and miserable. Zoshia found an inner resolve to be strong and courageous. She was happier when nightfall covered them with its dark veil. Zoshia knew that Pierre was familiar with the route and felt comforted by that. Encouraging the children with smiles, hugs and praise, all executed in whispers, Zoshia hoped that this would melt the ice of death which might envelop them. They walked and walked till nightfall. Zoshia ensured that her charges kept up. She did not want these children, who were blossoming seeds of life, to experience the worm of death. It was very difficult trudging through the snow, yet the children, aware of the dangers ahead, never complained.

Suddenly there was a gunshot. Then another. Then several all at once! Had they been discovered? How? No one knew they were there. Unless someone had spotted them leaving the station and heading into the depths of the forest. Pierre told them, "Align yourself with the branches and... pretend you are one of them," he added with a smile on his face, as though he was suggesting a game to play, and certainly not as if their lives depended on it. "I don't think they have any dogs with them, so we are in luck," he whispered to Zoshia with hope and encouragement.

"Quiet, little ones," Zoshia mouthed to the tree absorbed youngsters who had blended with nature like primitive creatures naturally content in their habitat, but hardly daring to breathe. Zoshia's heart was beating as if she was running in a race. This was a race for life and she prayed for salvation. They weren't going to die, and she defied fate to allow this to happen to these innocent children. She wanted them all to live. They were so young and did not deserve to have their lives exterminated in this way. As the soldiers moved nearer towards them, they splayed their torches in different directions in the hope that they would find someone. Suddenly there were thunderous shots and shrill voices shrieking. The Nazis had begun to chase some foxes. All the soldiers followed to where the sounds were coming from. It was as if they believed that other refugees were trying to escape. They ran off in the opposite direction. Pierre signalled to everyone to remain where they were in case the soldiers returned. It was a blessing they did not bring any dogs and that foxes in the woods created a lifesaving distraction.

"OK, let's move on," Pierre instructed, in a false jovial fashion as the children clamoured gingerly out of the trees.

They trampled hurriedly through the snow as faces were numbed with the icy bitterness. As the days went by, the journey seemed never-ending and rations were low. Some of the younger ones whimpered with exhaustion. Zoshia had to be strong for all of them. At one point she had to carry a tiny child on her back for some of the trek, as they could not risk stopping. They knew that the Nazi soldiers might appear at any moment, but they hoped that this would not be the case. Zoshia was amazed at her own strength and she was grateful for the training that she had been given. "Oh, please how much further?" the children asked repeatedly.

"Not too far now," Zoshia frequently replied, trying to keep them calm. Suddenly they heard noises, voices and gunshots. "Oh no, they're here!" Zoshia cried.

Pierre picked up two children. "We are nearly there, but we will have to take this route which is extremely dangerous. Run! Run as fast as you can!" he ordered, urgently. Pursued by Nazi soldiers, Zoshia, Pierre and their charges reached the edge of a twenty-foot ravine. As it was dark, it was difficult to see the depth. For all of them, except Pierre, it appeared to be a huge hole covered with snow. "Jump – Now!" Pierre commanded. They all jumped.

They landed in deep, soft snow and stayed there hidden. No soldier would take that leap as it was too high and too risky. The Nazis left, having presumed that everyone was dead. No one moved. Silence. No one was hurt. Pierre had known before they had jumped exactly where they were. He knew that this dangerous leap would not have been possible without the soft snow to break their fall. Pierre's plan to escort the children via a different route had been thwarted by the German soldiers and the ravine had been their only option. Now they had landed across the Swiss border where a resistance worker was waiting, on duty. "Welcome to Switzerland! You are safe now. Follow me," he said jovially. They all followed out from the darkness into the misty dawn of light and the morning rays of safety.

Zoshia hoped and prayed that she would be allowed to remain too.

The children were told they would be able to stay with families offering to host them before the Swiss Secret Service would take them inland to seek asylum. Zoshia, at sixteen years old, was refused entry. Although thoroughly disappointed, she was delighted that her children were safe. Returning through the woods was just as dangerous but she trusted Pierre implicitly and the journey, though daunting, made her realise that she would continue to help the Jewish children as long as she was able to. Zoshia continued with Pierre to help many of them to escape undetected into Switzerland until she had to return to her family for good. They were moving on.

Smule showed his pride and joy when he saw Zoshia again. He admired her heroism but inwardly was relieved that she had come back permanently to him in one piece. Each time she had left on a mission, Zara and Smule had been overcome with anxiety. This was the lifestyle that the Freedman family had become used to as the war progressed. In order to survive, they moved across France to a number of different hiding places supported by the French Resistance Movement.

Smule and Zara decided to return to Belgium in July 1944 as they heard that the allies were making progress in defeating Hitler's army. They took refuge in Brussels in an apartment in Avenue Louise near to the Gestapo Headquarters. It was a huge risk but surely the Nazis would never suspect Jews to be living nearby, almost at their front door. The representatives from the Belgian Resistance in

Brussels brought them food and necessary supplies to sustain the meagre life they were leading. From the attic window they could see the German soldiers entering and leaving the headquarters across the road. Zoshia would plead with her father, "Oh Papa, will we not be discovered here? We are just too close."

Smule replied empathetically. "It is a risk, I agree. Life is a risk in these dreadful times, but we can't keep moving. Your mother is very weak, and she needs some stability, Zoshela." He knew his daughter was right but felt powerless to do anything else at this time.

However, the inevitable happened. Their dreaded nightmare was realised when from their garret room they heard a fierce knock at the front door. "This is the end, Papa. Someone must have betrayed us," Hannah shrieked in terror and Smule covered her mouth to silence her.

"Offne die tier!" shouted a loud, harsh, authoritative voice. This was followed by the sound of two ferocious Alsatian wolfhounds, snarling and growling urgently, smelling out their prey. Smule whispered intensely, "We must go now! Immediately! We are at the mercy of those evil beasts if we stay. Let's go! Quick! Quick!" The silence of their escape was roaring as the four desperate fugitives stealthily clambered down the external, spiral steps at the rear of the building, having left a radio on loudly. The Nazi hunters entered aggressively through the front door which was opened by the owner of the house Alfons Wouters, who deliberately took as long as he could to answer their knocking. "Je viens. Un moment s'il vous plait," he stuttered in fear of his life. As the SS entered the building, they pushed Alfons out of the way and searched the house, room by room. It took them several minutes before they reached the top of the inner staircase to the attic. For some blessed reason it did not occur to the soldiers to scour outside; instead they started ransacking the attic room for the victims. Meanwhile the hunted animals were able to escape. Having been unable to find the Jews they had been looking for, the soldiers began to shout loudly; the dogs growling; guns shooting aimlessly yet threateningly as they ran all over the house and into the street. The desperados had fearfully fled from this horror and took shelter at the back of a bakery shop, which was owned by a secret resistance worker. Had they been caught, it would have been instant death by shooting or a slow death at a concentration camp. They had been spared by a higher force and they all prayed with tears of gratitude streaming down their faces.

The pressure on their lives continued to take its toll on the Freedmans. They lived in constant fear; they ate meagre rations and were continually moving to different hiding places. Living on the verge of discovery at any time was exhausting and terrifying. Smule and Zara's health began to deteriorate. But this nomadic lifestyle was to be their saviour as Zoshia and her family survived the war and returned to Antwerp in 1945 to rebuild their shattered lives. Zoshia would often say in the future that they survived because they had constantly moved around and that others were killed because they stayed in only one hiding place and were eventually betrayed and discovered.

"How will we recover from this experience?" Zara asked her husband mournfully.

"We never will," he replied blankly. "We never will," he repeated with the same monotone sound to his voice. Their gift of survival had been transformed into guilt for being alive. Their suffering, although a nightmare could not compare with those who had experienced the death camps.

Zoshia would continually ask, "Why were we selected to continue living when so many others had died?" Zoshia would never be able to put this thought out of her mind. It was a question no one could answer and it would haunt her always.

The effects of their years of persecution was plain to see. Zoshia had not experienced a normal teenage life; Hannah, now a young woman, had no positive memories and Smule and Zara suffered continuous ill health. For Zoshia, feelings of panic and worry often took hold of her and all her dreams were nightmares in which she relived those years of suffering and terror. She constantly feared the authorities. She was unable to confide in her parents as they still lavished their attention on a demonstrative Hannah. Despite the war having ended, Zoshia still felt separate; something her father tried to avoid all those years ago when he left Poland. And she still felt unloved by her mother. Zoshia hated this feeling and was determined to become strong and take control of her life. She would pray for courage.

Grace 4

During the war years, Grace loved her life with her Aunt Margaret and Uncle Peter, safe from strife. It was a little corner of the world where, for the first time in her life, she was happy. Her parents stayed in Harpenden with her brother, George, and sent the odd letter to Margaret (never to Grace directly) with money for Grace's upkeep. Grace pursued her passions and nurtured her talent for drawing and ballet, the latter being her true love. She adored her ballet teacher. Mrs Ellison, knowing that the child had an innate ability, continued to push her to her limit. Grace practised tirelessly and with dedication every day. At this time everything was just as it should be for Grace. She loved her aunt and uncle, who doted on her and serviced her every need. They continually praised her efforts in the arts and the child blossomed.

The effects of war were not damaging to young, eleven year old Grace. Her relationship with her aunt and uncle gave her a sense of security she had not felt before. She was free to play with her friends on the edge of the beach and search gleefully through the rocks for different sorts of sea creatures. Grace would fill up her little pink bucket with the world. On one occasion while searching under the boulders, she heard tremendous roars emerging from the sky. Grace saw crowds rushing and running in different directions. The screams were as loud as the roars that had caused them. "We are being invaded," somebody shouted. "Quick! Hurry! Let's get to safety," screamed another voice. During the panic, Grace was trying to hide. She wasn't frightened and thought of it as a game. She ran with her friend Polly and hid underneath a boat while giant birds flew overhead. They sat and giggled under their protective shelter, not realising the danger they were in. Eventually the sounds grew dim. No bombs were dropped. The two girls clambered out from their hideaway and ran homeward. Grace heard Aunt Margaret's voice calling out to her, "Oh, my goodness, you're safe." Though not a woman to raise her voice, she was overjoyed to find her little niece safe and gave Grace an affectionate tight hug.

The war had caused separation for the Brookfield family. Edward and Jean did not want to evacuate their children to strangers like many families were forced to do. They were secure in the knowledge that Grace was safe with Margaret and Peter. Not wanting to be parted from George, Jean had insisted that she would be able to protect him. This had been the best option for them all, despite the fact that imminent threat of German invasion was always lurking like a savage beast waiting to spring on its prey. Edward was hounded by a constant feeling of inferiority as he had been prevented from enlisting in the army due to his weak left arm. He compensated for this by his bullying tactics. He seized every opportunity to dominate someone, particularly his daughter. It made him feel in control and gave him a stronger sense of his masculinity.

It was now the summer of 1944 when Grace's parents visited with George, who was eight years old. This abruptly took Grace out of the idyllic world she shared with her aunt and uncle. The atmosphere completely changed. There was a coldness which purveyed the air and Grace once more turned inwards. She would receive criticism from Edward, who would besmirch her free and easy appearance. "Why can't you be smart like your brother?" he moaned. George just sat in silence. He was a quiet, sullen boy who never ever revealed his emotions. He was tall, slim and never smiled. He could speak but this was a rare occurrence. His grey eyes gazed downwards, and his hands were always crossed, one over the other. His downturned lips seemed to convey a miserable ambiance to his demeanour. No one ever really knew what he was thinking.

"You always seem to be running outside to play with the other urchins. If you don't stop these distractions and stay inside to practise your ballet, I will stop paying for your lessons," Edward added vehemently. Grace resented his constant denigration and she suppressed her growing anger which was bubbling like a dormant volcano about to erupt. "Why does father have to be so cruel to me?" she would mutter, tormentedly to herself. When her tormentor and his family eventually returned to Harpenden, Grace breathed a sigh of relief, though felt guilty at her feelings of elation.

Grace did not realise how lucky she was living in Lyme Regis which was not subject to the same dangers as London and the home counties where bombs were dropped and the tube stations used as air-raid shelters. Lyme Regis did, however, endure the deafening planes flying overhead like gigantic swarms of bees. The German bombers used the Cobb Harbour as a marker. When they reached it as they traversed the channel, the planes turned towards whichever destination they were going to. While it was frightening for families to hear these planes, it was not as serious as it might have been. Yet it was the unknown which was the primal fear.

One night, when the encircling planes were flying overhead, there were also dark clouds of thunder rampaging across the sombre sky. Grace peeked through the curtains in her bedroom to see that her moon was hidden. Grace was told her blackout curtains should always be shut tight, but she was unable to resist watching the moon when she could; it was her friend and brought her comfort. Suddenly, a flash of lightening stabbed savagely through the heavy haze of darkness. Grace jumped! She was shocked at the force and power of the storm. The world seemed to shudder and shake; the wind and rain caressed her window as nature quivered in sorrow while the giant fiends flew menacingly overhead. Margaret checked in on her charge, whose face was white, and her body frozen in shock. "It's alright, pet. Don't worry. It's just Mother Nature's way." Grace felt comforted and when her aunt put her into bed, she prayed that she could stay with her aunt and uncle forever. As her eyes closed, she told herself that she would see her moon tomorrow and contentedly fell asleep as Margaret tiptoed softly out of the room and gently closed the door. The planes moved on and the storm abated.

Peter and Margaret continued to care for Grace. Peter, like Edward, had not been accepted into the army due to a serious case of tuberculosis as a child, which left him with a permanent weakness in his chest. Grace's aunt and uncle continued to provide the love and comfort which she had been missing. She would dance for them and relished the applause she received at the end of her performances.

"Well done! Bravo! You dance like an angel," declared Uncle Peter, with much enthusiasm as he gazed at his niece with admiration. Grace would smile happily, her face blushing as red as a beetroot. She felt closer to her aunt and uncle than she did her own parents. Growing up, she had never known the warmth and comfort of physical affection and she loved the hugs that Uncle Peter gave her, which were strong and comforting.

Grace loved to play in the barn and her uncle would secretly watch her as she stared through the skylight fantasising about performing as a ballerina on a huge stage. Everyday Grace would climb the ladder in the barn just beyond the farmhouse. Lying down on the straw, she would feel its crispness next to her skin. She loved the natural texture of the straw, almost like a young animal lying in its nest. Some days she would stare at the clouds drifting past, dreaming lazily of faraway lands.

On one of these daydreaming excursions in her thirteenth year, she was aware of the sound of footsteps slowly being pressed on the rungs of the ladder. Who was it? Peter had tried to climb the ladder silently to watch his beautiful young niece lying there innocently with her blonde, unkempt curls aligning themselves to the shape of the straw, while her aquamarine eyes stared above her. Grace noticed that Uncle Peter was standing over her looking down at her from a great height. She smiled and felt safe in his presence.

"Hello, Uncle. What are you doing here?" Grace asked inquisitively. "This is my special place. How did you find me?"

Peter knelt down beside her and quietly and slowly began to caress her. "Shush, sweetie," he replied in a breath laden voice. Grace wasn't worried about her Uncle Peter showing her affection as it made her feel secure. He put the weight of his body upon her. He was a big man. Grace began to wonder now what he was trying to do.

"Uncle Peter, you are heavy. Please don't." She could smell his breath close to her and she felt nauseous. His breathing became more intense as he writhed about on top of her slight body. She tried to push him off her but was helpless to do so. He tried to kiss her on the mouth. He started to touch her. "No, Uncle Peter, I don't want to," she cried helplessly. "Please stop!" So far, she had been static in her response but now she knew this was wrong. Grace began to wriggle and scream. He covered her mouth with his hand and she screamed against it as if her whole life depended on it. Miraculously, this worked and Peter lifted himself off her and silently slipped away down the ladder, leaving Grace shocked and shaken. She felt completely ashamed, believing she had done something wrong and vowed not to tell anyone. How could Uncle Peter behave in this way? She loved him so much and he had betrayed her. Crying uncontrollably, she buried her head deep into the straw and gripped it with her fingers, clutching and bellowing like a wounded animal.

After a while Grace stopped crying. She wondered whether she had dreamt the whole episode. Having no understanding or experience of life, this came as an absolute shock. Why? Why would he do this? The rivers of anguish flowed down her hot flushed face. She felt she could not tell anyone and the best thing would be for her to run away where no one would be able to find her. Clambering down the step ladder, Grace stealthily slipped away from the barn and began to run as if her life depended on it. Uncle Peter's eyes were in front of her eyes and she could still feel his breath on her face. As she passed some cows in the field, she thought they looked at her as if they knew exactly what had happened. After what felt like an eternity of running, Grace arrived at a neighbouring farm, one mile away, where she rested. There was no hunger or thirst, as her tormented mind took control of her being. Hiding in the long grass, she could see what a perfect place this seemed to be. School boys were picking potatoes so innocently and one boy placed a couple into his pocket. She could hear the cows being milked inside the barn. A horse and cart drove by ready to collect the crates of milk. The sounds of dogs barking and chickens clucking noisily drowned her inner torment, when suddenly a black and white sheep dog ran up to her with warmth in its eyes. Looking at it's collar, Grace found his name; Cracker. She hugged him and immediately began to feel at ease. I want to stay here, Grace thought to herself. She stroked and embraced the dog as if by doing so she was bringing herself back to life. She lay down and promptly fell asleep.

Aunt Margaret had become very concerned about Grace's disappearance. She was used to her wandering off, but this had been far too long. Praying that nothing had happened to her niece, she relayed her fears to her husband. He was unusually quiet but said nonchalantly, "I'm sure she will be back soon. Don't worry." Margaret took notice of her husband, but she could not dispel her anxiety. As the hours passed, she insisted that they should go and search for Grace. They went in different directions; Margaret went inland and Peter searched seaward. After one hour, they both returned home without success. "We will have to telephone Edward and tell him what has happened, Peter," she sobbed. Sitting down to pick up the phone, Margaret heard a knock at the front door. She put the phone down and hesitantly opened the large wooden door, fearing it was the police.

"Our dog, Cracker, found her you see," said a gentle voice from the next farm – Mr Oakwood. "She was asleep in the grass." Grace stood there with her head hanging down. She was covered with dry grass and looked very unkempt. She did not dare to look up.

"Thank you very much for bringing her to us. We are so grateful. Thank you," uttered Margaret, wondering why Peter had walked back into the kitchen. "My poor lamb. We were just about to phone your father to tell him you were missing. No need to now, pet. You must be starving. Go upstairs and clean yourself up and I will bring you up something to eat. We will say no more about it. You are safe at home and that is all that matters." Grace could not look at her aunt and went to her room. After scrubbing herself clean, she sat motionless on the edge of her bed. She felt like a zombie. Emptiness. Nothing else. There was a knock on the door and Grace rapidly jumped up like a frightened hare onto her feet. "I have your supper ready. Can I bring it in?" her aunt requested softly. No reply. Margaret gently opened the door. "Eat this, and go to sleep. You can tell me all about it tomorrow after you have slept," she added in a mild tone. Closing the door behind her, Grace's aunt crept down the stairs. Feeling hungry, she demolished the meal. Having nourishment helped restore her. She told herself that she would never tell anyone about her horrific experience. Never.

Just after Grace's private battle had happened, World War II ended in 1945, and Grace prepared to return to her parents in Hertfordshire. She did not want to be back with her dominating father, but she knew that it was certainly the lesser of two evils. She was dreading going back to his criticism and cruelty. Grace had known what it was like to live in a house where there was serenity, peace and love but even this was a lie. Maturing into adulthood, she felt that she had been betrayed and taken advantage of by Uncle Peter. No, she must not dwell on that, she told herself. She would go home and pretend once more that everything was alright and withstand her father's lectures through gritted teeth.

To her surprise and delight Edward and Jean had bought Grace a puppy – a Yorkshire Terrier which was ready and waiting for her when she arrived home. She was thrilled to have something of her own to love. "I'm going to call her Honey because she is so sweet," Grace chuckled with delight and promptly took her upstairs to her bedroom. She stroked Honey for some time, as she sat on her tweed carpet.

However, the clouds began to gather around her as vivid images of her uncle appeared once more. The delight and innocence of her childhood had been stripped mercilessly from her, leaving only sadness and devastation.

Anticipation and excitement reigned in Britain as people celebrated the end of the war. There was singing, dancing, fireworks and bonfires. The heroic soldiers returned from war to crowds of cheers and applause. Edward and his family went to pay their respects as the soldiers appeared triumphantly before them. Edward saw himself as a complete outsider and intense envy and feelings of self-loathing overtook him. The injured arm which had prevented him from joining the army weighed heavily on him as he watched the victorious and conquering soldiers' jubilance. Edward felt that his masculinity had been threatened.

Following this excursion, Edward's dominance over his daughter was exacerbated. He ensured that Grace would adhere to his every wish. When she asked if she could go to the cinema with her friends, this was utterly forbidden. "No daughter of mine will behave in such a way. I do not want a child of mine corrupted," Edward ascertained. Grace was only permitted to listen to certain music that befitted a young lady and would only be allowed to attend the theatre or opera performances with her parents.

Crying inconsolably into her pillows every night, she felt friendless, forgotten and forsaken. Her despair was partly because of Edward's dominance but she was also distraught about her experience with Uncle Peter. Sometimes she felt physically sick thinking about it. Her weeping was something Grace was powerless to prevent. Eventually it was Jean who noticed how sad her daughter appeared, with her swollen red eyes permanently filled with water. She asked her daughter why she was so constantly troubled. Her unusual empathetic tone gave Grace some courage. Could she tell? Should she tell? It would be such a relief to confide in her mother who would surely understand. "You see, it was Uncle Peter... he tried to touch me... Oh his breath... he was heavy!"

Sobbing hysterically, Grace confided every aspect of her ordeal expecting sympathy and comfort. But her mother responded in disbelief. "No Grace, this is not true!" as she slapped her violently across her cheek. "This could not possibly have happened! Either you have made this up or YOU have behaved abnormally in some way! I am speaking to your father at once!" Jean raised her voice to a crescendo which Grace had never heard before and it terrified her. Dumfounded, she could not comprehend how her own mother would think that she was lying about something like this. She sat motionless and horrified in disbelief. Honey nibbled her foot wanting attention, but Grace did not notice her affection.

When Edward received the news from his wife, the anger which enveloped his whole being resurrected his own childhood memories, when he had been left motherless. His anger and his resentment surfaced and was projected on to his lying, conspiring slut of a daughter. Despite his best efforts, she was just like his mother, Beatrice. Confronting Grace with her evil lie, Edward stared coldly at her when she proceeded to tell him about her ordeal. As she spoke, she could sense the disbelief in his face. Although his features appeared motionless, he was completely immune to her tears and stated icily, "Have you finished?" Grace looked at the floor which was like a well of water around her. Edward said nothing more. He went upstairs where Honey was playing with a ball of wool and picked her up. With the puppy in his arms he coldly told his daughter, "We are returning her to the original owner. You do not deserve any pleasure after the way you have behaved, Jezebel!"

"Oh no, please, please don't take her," she pleaded. "I need her so much," and she fell prostrate on to the cold damp floor. Edward and Joan ignored their begging child and closed the front door after them. Grace went up to her bedroom and hid under her covers. She was safe in her own world. No one could harm her in the warmth of her cocoon.

The next few days passed, and quiet emptiness filled the house. Grace was unable to speak. It was as if the howl inside her could not escape. The silence was so loud, it was preventing her from action. On the third morning after the revelation, while Grace was eating breakfast with her family, there was a knock at the door. "It will be them," Edward said to his wife. "George, go up to your room," his father commanded. "Don't come down until you are called." George silently obeyed.

Grace began to shiver as four people entered the room. She looked up meekly and noticed two men and two women. They were a group of Edward's very close friends. After having approached them, they agreed to help for support. He had not told them the true details of his daughter's imagined story, fearing the shame it would bring to his family's name. Instead, he said it was a private family matter but that she had been lying about something completely unforgivable and that he needed their help to persuade her to admit her deceit.

"Grace, stand up," ordered Mr Thomas, who appeared to be in control.

"Do as you are told, girl," Edward added in a frustrated tone. Grace forced herself to her feet. Her knees were shaking. She wanted to go to the toilet. "Please can I be excused," she asked quietly.

"Stay where you are. Don't move," her father sternly responded. Grace put her trembling knees together at the sound of his agitated voice.

"Now, Grace," Mr Thomas said with a gentler tone, "it is forbidden to tell lies, is it not?"

"Yes, sir," Grace replied, barely audible.

"Then why are you lying to your family?" Miss Hardbattle challenged menacingly.

"Grace, you must admit that you are lying," said Mr Drake with force in his words.

"Young lady, confess that the story you told to your parents is untrue, at once," added Miss Montgomery as they all veered towards their charge who had strayed.

"Tell us it was all lies, Grace," they uttered loudly in unison. "Confess you have been lying and show some remorse and atone for your imaginings." Grace looked penitent. She collapsed in a heap on the floor, sobbing and said nothing.

Mr Thomas told Edward that Grace's face appeared to show repentance and that their job was finished. All she needed to do was vocalise it, which she was more likely to do privately rather than in front of strangers. Edward showed them out while Jean told her daughter to go upstairs and wash herself clean. When Grace left the room, Jean mopped up the puddle which had been left on the floor.

Well aware of Grace's silence her father decided to put up the shutters on the whole incident. He did not want anyone discovering what had been said and the dreadful behaviour which his child had displayed on her return from Lyme Regis. Edward did not confront Grace about the subject. She was told that the matter would not be referred to again, ever.

Grace felt desolate and alone. She knew that she would have to put this ordeal behind her if she was to survive. George would never believe her, and Aunt Margaret would think she had imagined it too. So, for now she vowed to try and live her life and suppress the memory of this dreadful experience. The elders upset her utterly and she could not believe that her father would have organised something so heartless. It was not her fault; it was Uncle Peter's fault. She had not imagined it or fabricated lies. She realised it was time to find some strength from within – she had to. Having already built a safety net of resilience and isolation around her, Grace vowed to be stronger, hoping that she would become as powerful as a man, so that her father would not be so disappointed in her as a young woman. She desperately wanted to make her parents believe that she could be a better person; a person they could love.

Zoshia 5

The devastating effects of the war had left the Freedman family totally damaged. Having endured an agonising, traumatic lifestyle and constantly fearing for their lives, they found it impossible to forget their past, and struggled to adjust to a normal life. The initial excitement and the street celebrations allowed them to forget for a while. The crowded streets, full of people shouting and screaming uncontrollably with joy, were a contrast to the agonising yells of Jews being physically persecuted and hounded like dogs by the German soldiers. Drums were beating loudly; music and singing accompanied the jostling. The jumping and the tremendous delirium of delight continued for days. "Isn't it wonderful, Mama, Papa, that the war is over? The Germans have gone! We are free to go outside! I can't believe it. We have survived!" Zoshia yelled, as loudly as she could.

"Yes, Zoshia, yes,yes,yes!" her parents replied joyfully, with as much excitement as they were able to express through their immense physical deterioration.

While contemplating their good fortune at having withstood the horrors of war and having lived through the persecution, a surprise awaited the Freedman family. There was a loud ring of the bell of their apartment. Fear was never far away. Zara opened the door and froze. Her eyes could not believe what she saw. With her heart racing, she screamed as loud as she could, as the rest of the family stood by her. Tears appeared in Smule's eyes. Zoshia and Hannah looked at each other as they could not fully understand what was happening and who these people were. They stared at three ghostly skeletons standing in front of them: emaciated bodies. They looked like coat hangers on which their clothing limply hung. These desperate wretches stood facing them. It was as if these three people were from another world; one of cruelty, injustice and torture and words could not appear on their lips because of this. Zara mumbled, "Leon, my Leon. Is it really you? Oh Rosa, I can't believe it! You're alive! I thought you were murdered! I didn't think you would be here on my doorstep. Oh come in. Come in. You are safe." Silence. There was no reply, just cascading tears as each of them held and caressed the other.

Zara's brother, Leon Kratawski, and his wife, Rosa, and their fifteen-year-old daughter, Gita, had survived living in the Warsaw Ghetto and had escaped the horror of the concentration camps. They were starving but had managed, with the help of gentile friends, to escape from Poland and travel to Belgium in search of their family. And now they were there and could be nourished and would sleep to try and recover, at least physically. Zara and her family took care of her relations until they would feel strong enough to talk. For the time being, there would be no questions. Zara's brother was alive. He had saved his wife and daughter and was in Antwerp. Though Zara and Smule were both very weak they found enough energy to help Zoshia and Hannah care for their newly-found love ones.

Days after Leon, Rosa and Gita's arrival, they listened intently as Leon described their experiences while Poland was held captive and under German occupation. As far as Leon was aware, all of Smule and Zara's relatives, living beings with hopes and dreams, had been destroyed by war. Their ashes had become dust. Recalling this, Leon's words became mingled with tears as his frozen heart burned, while weeping for the death of their loved ones who had been sent to Treblinka and now their departed souls were just dust in the wind.

"In 1940 the Warsaw Ghetto had been created and all Jews had to be relocated to this part of Warsaw. All our families had been transported there. There was also a gentile section which did not have the same restrictions as Jews. Rooms were so cramped, Smule, with eight of us sharing one room. We weren't allowed many possessions; just the necessities. Thank goodness that my good friend Franciszek Novak agreed to look after my savings when we Jews were forced into the ghetto, Zarala. However, while I was in the prison city, it did not seem to matter then. We were all poor and destitute. People tried to smuggle food. Our meagre diet was bread, sawdust and potatoes," said Leon still sighing with suffering at his memory.

"We suffered too, Leon, when we led our nomadic life trying to avoid the German dogs," she added. "It was not like you. The Germans didn't find us, although it was very close," Zara continued while shivering.

"My poor Zara," Leon responded. "Everyone was starving – children were dying in the streets. Typhus was rife. Thousands of Jews died from starvation. It was so cruel. The suffering, the hunger, the torture. It was a slow death for so many. The blanket of misery and wretchedness hung like a shroud. It was Hitler's plan, you see, Smule. He wanted the ultimate destruction of dangerous groups as part of his plan to purify the Aryan race. He believed that from all the drops of blood that were spilt, this race would become the jewel of existence. No one could escape or even try, as the punishment would be instant death. Later, Zoshia, there was the mass deportation of Jews to the Treblinka death camp where our Jewish relatives perished in the gas chambers. Oh Smule," Leon wailed, "I wish I could have been sensible like you and had left Poland before the war started."

"Leon," Smule responded sympathetically. "You couldn't have known what would happen.

"Many of us still remained in the ghetto and people worked for German-run companies. I managed to join the Jewish Police Force so that I could be less intimidated. It was a terrible experience as it appeared that I was betraying my fellow man. I wasn't. I was trying to survive. It was because of this role that I eventually managed to escape with Rosa and Gita, as I had to accompany the lorries through the gates and when outside, I jumped into the lorry where my family was already hidden, having been helped by other members of the Jewish Police. We were cared for by Catholic nuns until representatives of the resistance organised our journey to Belgium, at my request. My nightmares are visions of dead children lying in the streets of the ghetto as German soldiers kicked them out of their way. People begged for help but survival of the fittest was the order of the day. At least we escaped the death camps and I pray with thanks everyday that we were saved. Defeat is not declared when you fall down, only when you can't get up. We managed to rise from the ashes of suffering, somehow."

Leon, Rosa and Gita stayed for a while with Zara and her family until their own apartment was found. It was not very big, but it suited Zara's brother admirably. They were free and Smule loaned his brother-in-law enough money until he could receive his savings.

However, though they could all now continue with their lives, the years of physical hardship had seriously affected Smule and Zara's health. Zoshia and Hannah lived in fear of losing their beloved parents who were very weak. Luckily, Smule's dear old friend, Arvin Van de Vijver, a Gentile friend, had supported him with his business accounts prior to the start of Hitler's invasion and promised to take care of the money Smule had made before the war. This money now helped Zoshia and Hannah to look after their parents. Smule seemed to have lost a sense of himself and had aged. Zara went through the motions of daily routines automatically, as if her life depended on her cooking, cleaning and shopping. At least her brother was close and this comforted her. She executed commonplace everyday things, which she hoped would make her feel normal once more. She would continue to lavish praise on Hannah, even though she was now a young woman, so that she would not argue with her younger sister.

Zoshia had kept that tiny photograph of herself with her friends which had been taken before the war. She stared in dismay at the photo of all the girls smiling joyfully at the camera. Her tears blotted out each child's face, mimicking ironically the disappearance of them all. Killed. Dead. Every single one of them had been transported to the extermination camps together with their families. Zoshia could not comprehend why she had been selected to survive. What had she done to deserve being allowed to continue her life? She sobbed and felt so very lonely and isolated without the comfort of her friends. She said a prayer for each of the eight souls: Regine, Anna, Betty, Sarah, Annette, Maya, Shira and Esther.

Time passed but Zoshia still felt her inferiority. Something inside her still felt unable to belong. She would watch how Hannah seemed to be the centre of her parents' world. Her sister had started dating several different young men, but no one could ever reach her high standards, and this contributed to Hannah's erratic mood swings. As she was constantly moaning to her parents, Zoshia felt unable to be part of their intimate talks.

The distraction which Zoshia needed came from her talent for languages. She had taken a test set by the Geneva University School of Interpreters as she was extremely fluent in German, French and English. She was delighted to have passed and she obtained a position as a translator at the Nuremberg trials.

Zoshia was told that she had to travel and stay in

Nuremburg so she could translate at the trial. Part of her was petrified at having to leave her household and travel to the country whose army had destroyed her whole extended family and friends by torture and murder. She had, however, experienced much danger herself during her time in France, so she knew that she could deal with travelling to Nuremburg. Smule and Zara did not want their daughter to leave but realised that what she was doing was important. They arranged for her to stay in a very small bed and breakfast hotel which was still standing after the war. Zoshia tearfully left them and took a train from Antwerp to Brussels and onward to Nuremburg in Bavaria. During the journey Zoshia stared out of the window at the vast countryside but could still not believe that she was free. Even when the train conductor came to check her ticket, Zoshia jumped and froze before she realised it was safe.

Nuremburg's old town was mainly devastated. Other parts of the city were heavily bombed by the allies. As she looked around, Zoshia could see the mass of destruction and rubble, where many buildings were in ruins; there were now merely bricks where once there had been majestic edifices; Zoshia noticed huge puddles of muddied water where people were trying to dig desperately for their belongings. The air was filled with green smoke emanating from the burnt and charred buildings, now just carcasses of debris and waste; fragments of a former life.

Zoshia eventually found where she was supposed to be staying and, speaking German, she could communicate easily with the landlady, Frau Lieberman. Climbing the stairs to her bedroom, Zoshia could hardly believe she was there and as she lay down on her bed in the tiny room, she promptly fell asleep.

In 1945 The Nuremburg trials were held for the purpose of bringing the Nazi war criminals to justice. The defendants included Nazi party officials and military officers of high rank along with German industrialists, lawyers and doctors. They were charged with crimes against peace and crimes against humanity. This was an early experiment in simultaneous translation. The Charter of the International Military Tribunal stated that the defendants had a right to a fair trial and so all proceedings would be translated into a language that the defendants understood. Zoshia became a valued part of these trials and this helped her to feel needed. At first she found it difficult to speak into the microphone at the same time as listening, but she soon became accustomed to what was required.

The accused faced the judges and there were German counsel and court reporters nearby. Zoshia was placed in a small, three-sided glass booth, which was extremely claustrophobic. She wore heavy clumsy earphones which were awkward, but she revelled in her job and so endured the uncomfortable sensations. The defendants would look at Zoshia and she did not hesitate to stare back at them with hatred in her eyes. This had a cathartic effect for her as she was able to see the perpetrators of the carnage stand trial for their crimes. Despite this satisfaction, Zoshia was always looking over her shoulder in case she would be 'caught'. She yearned to break free both physically and mentally from these feelings. The complete indoctrination of always having to run away was part of her psyche from which there was no escape.

The logical part of Zoshia knew that she was now safe as the war was over. But she was unable to dissipate her deep sense of fear. So much had happened. There had been no real personal happiness in her life. It was as if she had been living at sea in a boat without oars. The terror and horror that Zoshia had experienced would never leave her. SHE… she had escaped death. Death which was always too close and trying to engulf her being, could not reach her and now she was trying to live a new life.

One afternoon at the trials, Zoshia, deep in thought, entered the ladies' room to try and wash the perspiration from her face. The cool water immediately soothed her as she felt the icy liquid upon her skin. Reaching for a paper towel to dry herself, she could not help but overhear two cleaners who were speaking to each other in German. Zoshia nearly choked. No amount of water could eliminate the sweat that was soaking her body. She looked in the mirror. Her face was white. How could this be? The Nuremberg trials were safe. And yet…

Zoshia ran out of the toilets where the two women were still talking. Climbing the stairs with an urgency she hadn't felt since the war, she spoke to her friend Simon who was in the technology department. "I heard the two German cleaners talking… I could understand… they spoke about how… how they were… Aufseherin… in the camps. Yes those two female cleaners were guards in a concentration camp. I didn't hear which one. Please, please, please do something immediately."

Simon calmed Zoshia down briefly. "I will sort this out." And he promptly left. Tears flowed down Zoshia's face and flooded her eyes so that her vision was blurred and all she could see was a distorted view of the world. She had wanted to kill both of them but that impulse soon muted itself. When Simon returned, he tenderly informed her that the cleaners had been taken away for interrogation and questioning. Zoshia was extremely relieved and calmed down. She was here to do a job, a very important one. She had to take control despite the fact that she was still immersed in the war. Zoshia heard about so many disgusting atrocities that each day she would return home to her small apartment and cry. She prayed for some mental liberation from her daily perpetual torment, anguish and guilt at being alive. She needed something different; a distraction from her intense obsession over her war experience.

The salvation from her mental misery appeared in the form of Robert Ward, an English journalist who was working at the trials. She had noticed him in a local cafeteria, and she was immediately taken by his violet, blue eyes which were gazing at her from beneath his heavy, dark eyebrows. His strong, determined jaw seemed to emanate confidence and assurance. Zoshia felt embarrassed about her underlying sense of passion and sensations which were penetrating her body. She had never felt this way before. She was somehow comforted by her feelings. Each night, she would go to sleep having fantasised about their meeting and when she awoke, it was Robert who dominated her thoughts.

Robert Ward was a journalist who had been sent to Nuremburg to cover aspects of the trial. He was a well built, tall, muscular man, who exuded a friendly disposition due to an almost permanent fixed smile on his face. A caring human being, Robert felt privileged to be attending the trials. He had been in the army during the war and experienced horrors which would always remain in his psyche. Full of confidence, he loved to make people laugh but his serious mission in Nuremburg was of paramount importance to him. Robert had noticed this beautiful, shy, young woman sitting in the cafeteria and he was determined to get to know her. She seemed so mournful and reserved that she fascinated him.

At 1.05pm on a Thursday, Robert Ward approached Zoshia and asked if he could sit with her. She replied, "Yes, please do." She could feel her knees shaking and her heart fluttering so loudly, that she was certain he could hear it.

"I hope you don't think I'm being rude, but I have noticed that you come in here quite often, as I do and I hoped that you would allow me to buy you some dinner after we have finished work," he asked assertively.

"Yes, I would love to," Zoshia replied rather quickly. "I work as a translator at the trials, as I speak six languages you see: French, Flemish, German, Dutch, English and Yiddish," she added, trying to make him admire her

"Do you, indeed!" Robert responded, in such a way that Zoshia knew that he was impressed.

"One day I would like to have a career using these skills," Zoshia continued, feeling more confident.

"I am sure you will... I am a journalist from Windsor in England and I have been sent here to report on the trials, so I hope that we will be able to see a lot of each other," he declared in a slightly lower volume which conveyed his intelligence and magnetism. Zoshia was delighted that he had asked her. She loved his dark-brown hair and his handsome face and now she had been asked out to dinner and the offer of an exciting continuous form of relationship.

"I hope so too!" she replied, unable to hide her enthusiasm which seemed to delight Robert and completely surprise Zoshia.

The pair continued to meet regularly and discuss their lives with each other. Robert was horrified by Zoshia's stories of suffering and felt nothing but compassion for her tortured life. They were happy together and became very close. Zoshia felt elated most of the time because the sense of pleasure was so new to her. Someone liked her for who she was. He cared for her feelings and showed her respect and consideration. They laughed and talked together and it was not long before they knew that they had a powerful mutual love. Robert composed beautiful, romantic letters to her, proclaiming devotion. She kept his letters in her drawer in an old biscuit tin and would read them frequently. For the first time in her life, Zoshia felt real happiness. She would fall asleep, dreaming of Robert and would sleep peacefully, something which she had never done. In the morning, she would wake up with an excitement for a new day and looked forward to her life, loving each moment.

Zoshia could not reveal the relationship to her family. Robert was not Jewish, and she knew that they would never condone her having a close romantic connection with someone of a different religious background. Zoshia did not want to face this problem just yet. She was much too happy. The issue was put to the back of her mind as she wanted time to stand still, so that she could enjoy their love for as long as possible. She continued to ignore this unmoving obstacle, which she ultimately knew would eventually part them. She loved Robert deeply and a separation from him seemed too unbearable to contemplate.

Eventually, towards the ending of their time at the trials, it was Robert himself who created the inevitable confrontation. He proposed to Zoshia, despite knowing that their different faiths might be a problem, as they had discussed the difficulties they might encounter. "I love you, Zoshia. You are my whole world. Please, please be my wife," he implored, as they were sitting having dinner. "Let your life be flowered with love," Robert added sincerely. He loved her so much that the thought of losing her was inconceivable. Zoshia knew that she would never be able to marry him. Despite her traumatic suffering, Zoshia still believed in her faith and she felt compelled to obey its rules especially after all she had been through and because of it.

"My darling, I can't marry you. I will remember this moment forever. Please, please forgive me for hurting us," she pleaded, crying with hopelessness, but at the same time trying not to embarrass herself. Marriage to Robert would have been her dream, yet, despite his pressured persistence, the relationship ended that evening. Zoshia was alone once more and drinking from the cup of her own suffering.

Robert returned to England, a broken man.

Zoshia was devastated. What had she done? She felt that she had ruined both their lives. While Robert was with her, Zoshia felt whole and now there was nothing. Only emptiness. Her job at the trials was over and her year of love had finished too. Desolation encompassed her as a huge, black cloud. The intense heartache she felt was kept inside, as she was unable to confide in her parents. No one knew her excruciating pain and she found it extremely difficult to cover up her immense unhappiness, but she did. The only thing that cheered her was the fact that her parents' health had improved, although she knew that they would never be the same again. Zoshia had been like a caged bird who had been set free and now she was returning home to her family to beat her wings against the apparent captivity which would confine her to her birthplace once more. Having arrived at her parents' residence, life seemed unbearable as Hannah took centre stage with her problems. Having a romantic relationship with someone, and being away from home, Zoshia was less aware of Hannah's influence and her constant, continuous, criticism and torment. Now her suffering seemed relentless. She had to leave once more.

A huge decision was made. Smule's brother, Max Freedman, lived in London and it was agreed that Zoshia would stay with him and her Aunt Isobel. Leaving Antwerp for London allowed her to abandon the anxiety and suffering that she constantly felt. She hoped that staying in Britain's Metropolis would create an alternative future. This time, she told herself, she would truly escape.

Grace 6

Grace blossomed into a beautiful and creative eighteen-year-old young woman. She had continued with her ballet lessons and had appeared in many amateur performances. Still sustaining her dream of becoming a professional dancer, Grace practised every day. Her other passion was art and she continued to pursue her love of painting and drawing. Having passed her Higher School Certificate, she was offered a place at St Martin's School of Art in London. She had worked so hard at producing a portfolio of work to show them and now, at last, she truly believed that one of her dreams had come true.

When the letter arrived, she rushed in anticipation to open it. Having read it, she showed her father and mother who were eating breakfast. "I am so pleased. I have been accepted by St Martins Art School, father," she exclaimed, clapping her hands in excitement.

"Well, young lady. Listen to me. You have indulged yourself far too long. It's time you found an appropriate position that befits a daughter of mine. You are not going to mix with the worst in society at one of 'those' establishments," he stated, impassively yet emphatically. "I will not pay, nor will I pay for any more ballet lessons. Forget those ideas once and for all." He continued calmly to spread the jam on his toast, as he dispassionately destroyed Grace's dreams.

"But please, father! Please, please don't do this!" Grace cried. Her pleas fell on deaf ears, as her father and mother continued to eat their breakfast in silence. The stifling of Grace's needs was overwhelming. She felt persecuted and let down by her parents. She knew how much they had supported her brother and would never ever thwart his ambitions so hard-heartedly.

Out of loneliness, Grace joined a progressive Christian church in order to find comfort. With the people there, she found solace. At last she felt she belonged and was needed; a feeling that she had never experienced before. Grace was so happy to be able to join in with a community spirit. She made friends and no one questioned her. It was as if she was liked for who she was and she relished this new experience. This communal singing seemed to be intoxicating as the hosts of happy voices sang their immortal magic. Even this group of people were subject to criticism by Edward. Jean always nodded in agreement. She would never usually express a point of view. "You are trying to mix once again with unsatisfactory people. I am certain that the object of the exercise is for you to be able to flirt with the male members in the group," Edward remarked in an angry voice.

At this time and surprisingly, Jean added, "Grace, you're acting like a young floozie." Their daughter could not believe what was uttered from her parents' mouths. She could not reply. This was one of the many arguments that she had to endure, which made her feel utterly worthless; her misery growing more intense with each day.

It was nursing that gave Grace new hope. She was accepted by Westminster Hospital in London to train as a nurse. Grace was extremely delighted by this and it seemed that her father was satisfied with this choice of occupation; one which, he thought was suitable for a woman. She was sent to a children's ward where many young patients were suffering from tuberculosis. Grace found it extremely distressing yet ultimately rewarding. She would tend the sick children and help them to find some sort of comfort from their physical distress. A number of them inevitably died from the disease and every loss was hard for her to bear, particularly as she could not help becoming attached to them. This was something that she was told not to do but her heart ached for these helpless victims.

In her first year of studies, Grace excelled at the course which involved drawing aspects of the human body. Grace loved this part of the schedule and together with her obvious nursing skills, she achieved a distinction after the first year. Her life was seemingly falling into a pattern of contentment and progress but fate soon intervened and dealt Grace a crushing blow. The course became more difficult. Mathematics had always been difficult for her at school and despite studying earnestly and with dedication and commitment, she failed this part of the curriculum. Her failure was compounded by having to work in the men's wards, which she found embarrassing and upsetting. There was a feeling of bitter helplessness once more, even though she had tried so hard to succeed, particularly to please her father. She knew that others thought that she was a good and capable nurse but this was not enough.

Unfortunately, her feelings of insecurity gathered momentum when she became subjected to an attempted seduction by a senior night sister. Bertha Burke had noticed this slip of a girl for some time and hoped that in befriending her, they might become close. During a night shift, as Grace was washing her hands in the bathroom, Bertha entered and brusquely put her arm around Grace's waist. "We are friends, aren't we Grace?" Bertha uttered very softly, hoping for a positive response.

"Of course, we are friends," replied Grace innocently, though wondering why she needed to ask such a question. "Good girl," replied Bertha as she moved in closer and attempted to kiss Grace on the mouth. "What are you doing? No… Stop!" Grace shrieked. At this point Bertha left the room, leaving Grace dumbfounded.

For days afterwards, Grace felt as if she was in a mental stupor. There was no one she could confide in. Why would Bertha try to kiss her? Grace had never given her senior sister any affection other than as a friend. Hurt and confused, Grace made her decision about her career. She felt that this was the final straw in a year of great difficulty. She had to give up nursing. There were too many obstacles for her to overcome. She felt stripped of her initial success. Why did it have to come to this? Grace felt that she was being punished for no reason. She had always tried to be a good person and help others, but it seemed to her that there was no respite from personal suffering. This was a turning point in her life. When she told her father, he was cold in his response. "It seems, Grace, that you do not have the capability to amount to anything in your life. What a disappointment you are." Grace wept at her father's words. Emerging from within was a sense of hatred. She no longer believed that anyone or anything, despite her prayers, could help her. The only person she could rely on was herself. All her religious beliefs seemed futile and pointless, so Grace abandoned her faith.

Fortunately, she had managed to save some money and because of this Grace ultimately decided to leave the family home. "Go, you foolish girl. It might do you good to fend for yourself and realise all we have done for you. Yes, go!" Edward stated impassively and gave her a cheque. Their daughter was very grateful for this unusual display of support from her father. Jean said nothing. So, at the age of eighteen years old, Grace arranged to share a room with her school friend Moira with whom she had kept in touch. At school, Grace and Moria had been very close and this continued into adulthood. They would often talk on the phone and chat about their lives and their problems. Moria Mitchell was a girl with a very happy disposition. She was round in shape, but her large green eyes smiled on their own. Always caring about humanity, she showed genuine concern for her close friend's difficulties.

As she sat in her bedroom, Grace pondered her life with her family so far. Yes, she had been granted opportunities to study as she wanted but somehow, despite this, she had never felt the emotional love that a growing child needed from her parents. Materially, she had wanted for nothing and so she had never experienced financial hardship. But her unhappiness was compounded by the sorrow she felt with no physical love; no embraces; no praise; no encouragement. Despite this, she did love her mother and father and part of her was sad to leave them. Looking around the room that had been part of her life for so long, Grace felt anxiety overtake her whole being. The pretty yellow and green flowered wallpaper had been her companion every night as she traced the shapes of the flowers with her fingers. Grace remembered how, during her childhood, she had she stared at the brown wooden doors of her wardrobe and could see the patterning of the wood becoming lions' faces. She loved her green and yellow tweed carpet which she had kneeled on to do her drawings or to practise her ballet steps. This was home – her life – and now she was leaving to an unknown future. She knew she had to, as it was much too difficult living with her parents. Before she went to sleep that night, Grace opened the window to breathe in the fresh air as usual from outside. Staring at the navy sky, and the moon, which seemed to be smiling at her, Grace remembered many other nights, other skies and other moons. It was as if that sky had been a cloak that had shielded all her sorrows when she had looked at it throughout her young life. But now she was discarding it and hoping that her future would be daytime.

So, it was with much sadness that on a rainy morning she said goodbye to her father and mother to embark on a new part of her existence as a young, independent woman. Edward muttered that she should be very wary of others who might want to take advantage of her. He carried on reading his paper and did not look up. Jean accompanied her daughter to the front door and Grace was certain that she saw a tear in her mother's eye. "Goodbye, my dear. Keep your wits about you and remember all that we have taught you," Jean instructed solemnly. Her daughter walked with suitcase in hand to the bus stop trying with difficulty to remember what they had taught her.

With Moira, Grace moved to a guest house in Camden, London, which belonged to Moira mother's sister, Peggy. She was a kind-hearted, lovely woman who welcomed them both. Grace was very pleased to have this threshold of a new beginning where she could be herself, without the criticism from her father; the nonchalance of her mother and the uncaring attitude of her brother George, who had made no attempt to have any kind of sibling relationship with her. She had escaped. Freedom looked very inviting and exciting as she felt that the world was there for her at last to enjoy.

Zoshia 7

Zoshia could see that everywhere she went in London had been heavily bombed, and destroyed buildings were a familiar sight. Ariel bombings had devastated commercial districts and the industrial and residential parts of London. Bombardment affected the historical heart of the city and the port of London had been demolished and wrecked. Transport was reduced, which affected the availability food supplies. People were extremely shocked at the havoc that had destroyed a large number of buildings and which created shortages of all essentials and necessities. Many people were homeless or displaced. Despite the devastation that had been created, the war was over and everyone was grateful. Post-war London, seemed like paradise to Zoshia. She had escaped both mentally and physically from the external oppression that she had been subjected to all her life. Although she had not forgotten her beloved Robert, and never would, she felt that this was a new start for her. She had to be positive. This was a new country, with new people; a world that could open up endless possibilities.

Zoshia stayed in a small apartment near Regents Park, which belonged to her Uncle Max and Aunt Isobel Freedman, who had moved to London before the war. Max was also a very well-respected tailor and earned a good living making clothes for the elite in the city. He and Isobel had been fortunate to have missed the persecution in Europe yet unlucky to never have had children. They loved Zoshia and she was made to feel very welcome. Her aunt was an affectionate and kind woman who Zoshia felt she could confide in. Each day they would take long walks in Regents Park and Zoshia would look at the green gardens and the majestic lines of trees, which seemed to welcome her with their beauty. At one with nature she gradually began to heal her inner torment and though her pain would never be forgotten, Zoshia, felt strengthened and at peace.

However, she could not forget Robert, who was ingrained in her being. She remembered their mutual love for each other and the deliriously blissful times that they had spent together. His touch, his gentle touch. Oh how Zoshia wished that she could contact him. But no. The pain would be unbearable. She mustn't. Was being in England the reason why she felt so close to him? Strength was needed. No, she would use all her inner resilience to force herself not to think of him and, as the time passed, Zoshia felt herself thinking less and less about Robert and more about the future and how she could change her life.

Her relatives would often invite their friends for dinner and Zoshia would enjoy entertaining them by playing the piano. She adored the emotional music and delighted in the freedom of engaging an audience with her talent. She hoped that one day she would be able to achieve her ambition of being a concert pianist. On one such evening, her adept capability immediately captured the attention of a young doctor, Harvey Spencer. He had come to London from Liverpool at the invitation of his friends for the weekend. A General Practitioner, he had bought a surgery in the city having achieved distinction in his medical studies in Cardiff and had successfully completed years of training.

He had previously joined his brother Hayden in a practice in Tonypandy, South Wales, and together they had worked hard to build up a reputation. The local patients respected and admired them, but Harvey was restless. He wanted the freedom to run his own surgery and when he found one for sale in Liverpool he had jumped at the chance.

Having come from Bargoed, in the Rhonda Valley in South Wales, Harvey found it very difficult at first coming to live in a large city, where he knew very few people. Harvey was convinced, however, that he had made an excellent purchase and felt in his heart that he would earn a good living. A clever, intelligent man, who had a very caring nature, he would certainly make an excellent doctor for his future patients. For now, though, he was in London gazing at this beautiful girl, who clearly was much younger than he. Harvey was transfixed by her.

He was struck by her delicate beauty and an ethereal quality which she exuded by her smile as she played the notes on the piano with such intense passion and love. He too adored music; Chopin in particular. His love of playing the violin made him very aware of Zoshia's sensitivity. He had to meet and talk with her. Holidaying in London, he had been invited to Max and Isobel's home that evening with some friends of his: Emma and Nigel Pinkerton who had known Zoshia's aunt and uncle for many years. Fate has a way of affecting and changing lives and on this night, destiny dictated that Zoshia's life would be completely altered as she became entranced by the handsome, slightly older gentleman who stared so intensely at her with his mesmerising green eyes.

Harvey was introduced to Zoshia by Emma Pinkerton and it was easy to sense that their attraction to each other was, in an instant, magnetic. When he complimented her on her piano playing, Zoshia looked at him spellbound. Easy to talk to, she found Harvey comfortable to be with. As they chatted, time seemed to stand still. They discussed a mutual love of so many things; politics, literature but above all music. As Zoshia spoke fluent English, she was able to communicate with Harvey easily. Even though he had studied medicine at Cardiff University, his heart was always filled with the love of music. His father, Immanuel, and his mother, Ruth, had insisted that he should follow an academic route to a profession rather than pursue his love of music as a career. Like all his siblings, he was forced to work hard. Harvey had studied medicine and had become a doctor, but his true soul was elsewhere. When Zoshia played the piano, it was as if she was reaching into his deepest self. Her attraction to him was more than his outward appearance. She found his analytical mind fascinating and stimulating and she adored to listen intently to him speaking in his musical Welsh accent. Harvey was Jewish and this meant everything to Zoshia. There were no religious obstacles to overcome as there had been with Robert.

After two weeks had passed, Harvey left to go back to his medical practice in Liverpool and Zoshia departed for Antwerp to return once more to her family. This brief visit to London had proved to be more than she could ever have hoped for. After Robert, Zoshia thought she would never be able to fall in love again. However, she had met Harvey; someone who had enveloped her whole being. He had told her he loved her and she had reciprocated his feelings.

Zoshia returned to Antwerp a much more content person. Having left home, Zoshia felt that her world had come to an end! No one would have thought that she would meet another man who would open the doors to life once more as Robert had done. And yet here was Harvey, though much older in years, who had stirred something within her which she thought had died. She felt alive and finally had something to live for. While relating her experiences in London to her family, Smule and Zara were delighted to see the happiness radiate from their daughter. Hannah, though very envious of her younger sister finding love before she had, begrudgingly congratulated her. Yes, she felt resentful, but glad of her sister's joy.

"I love him so much," Zoshia told her parents, with an excitement she had never felt before. This time she could share her feelings with her family, which reinforced the validity of her emotions. Yes, the true love she had felt for Robert was powerful but this was even more intense and she did not have to question whether or not her family would approve because she knew that they too would feel a strong affection for him. The cards had been dealt and this time she had won the jackpot. The word happiness, which she had seldom been able to utter, had now overtaken her soul. This was why she had survived the horrific persecution, so that she could experience the meaning of true love. This was all that mattered.

"Zoshia, is that the doorbell?" Zara shouted as she stirred the goulash which she had prepared for lunch.

"I will answer it, Mushki," replied Zoshia who had just had a bath and had dressed herself ready for lunch. As she opened the door, she could hardly breathe. She could not speak. She pinched her arm tightly to check that she was not asleep dreaming this…

Harvey had travelled to Antwerp to surprise Zoshia and with the intention of asking Smule and Zara's permission to marry their daughter. He had been very anxious for the whole of his flight, constantly practising how he would first request Zoshia's parents to allow him to become her husband and then how he would propose directly to Zoshia herself. He loved her so much and could not imagine the rest of his life without her. He knew that coming to Antwerp was a terrible risk as he had not informed the Freedmans of his visit, or the purpose of his sojourn.

As she opened the door, Harvey blurted out, "If you don't agree to marry me, I will give up my medical practice and I would no longer wish to live. I love you to the depths of my soul. You cannot say no," he begged in earnest.

With tears falling down her cheeks, Zoshia slowly uttered in the affirmative voice, "Yes." They both knew that this would be for life, as they rushed to ask her parents' permission. Smule and Zara agreed immediately and were so happy as this handsome man was a perfect match for their precious daughter. Hannah smiled and wished them well, yearning inside to be the one who was planning a wedding.

Their wedding was a quiet affair and took place at the Hollandse Synagogue in Antwerp on the 28th July 1950. Harvey's family attended and Zoshia's family were present. Zoshia's uncle and aunt came over from London and the Pilkingtons attended as well. Zoshia was ecstatic and so grateful that she had found a true escape from her previously unhappy life. Now she had broken away from the continual dominance of her sister who had suppressed who she was. With Harvey, she knew that she would learn to become whole. To love and be loved; she was able to do this. She hoped to live happily in England and finally be free from the years of persecution she had endured during the Holocaust. She felt positive; a feeling that was new to her. At last Zoshia had real hope for the future.

Grace 8

Freedom tasted so sweet to Grace. Although she did not have much money, except for the small amount which her father had given her, she felt independent. There was enough to get by and she enjoyed the release from Edward's tyranny. Grace had found a job working in a flower shop, which she loved. Designing bouquets appealed to her creative sensibilities. It was inspiring to make choices of colours and shapes and compose them into the finished product. Grace felt very pleased when customers congratulated her on her arrangements. She was utterly content living in the guest house belonging to Moira's aunt. Peggy was an ample, cheerful woman with a large mop of curly red hair and a smile that consumed her face. She did not charge the girls too much rent and her cooked breakfasts were enough to satisfy the most ravenous appetite.

London life suited Grace. She loved to visit the numerous coffee shops and savour the coffee aroma and the friendly ambiance. Grace was intoxicated by the intense vibrant chatter and laughter. She found the smoke hazes that enveloped the rooms completely enticing. There was such intrigue when she listened to the groups of young beatniks, with their long hair and beards, discussing the arts. Gradually, after several visits, she started to sit with them directly and as her confidence grew, she gradually discovered that she had a voice and an opinion. Delighted with the responses she received and the respect her ideas conveyed, Grace at last felt her intelligent brain was being fed. Her isolation and sense of loneliness had diminished, and it was within these intellectual friendships that she found a sense of belonging. As a woman, she had started to feel a sense of parity with the male sex. Intellectually Grace was able express her views. It was her enquiring mind that impressed others as it was often difficult to respond to some of her obscure questions. The freedom to openly question ideas was exhilarating; throughout her life Edward had always prevented her from doing this and she had been forced to submit to his beliefs.

It did not occur to Grace to consider entering into a permanent relationship with anyone. She enjoyed her freedom, something which was new to her. However, there was the sound of her father's voice somewhere in the back of her mind, saying that she should be married before the age of twenty-one. It was unfortunate that she began to listen to this imagined comment more frequently, resulting in her attempting to analyse her male friends as potential husbands. Why did her father have such a strong influence on her? Was it because of his unmoveable adherence to the role of women in society as being subservient and not particularly important? She knew he looked down on women. Grace understood this was his subconscious anger at his mother leaving him and the power of the pain that controlled him as a result. Grace's generation understood their position was to be married at a young age and bear children and not to focus on their own potential as career women. Did she really want this role? Grace knew she was continually under the spell of her father's doctrine and therefore there was an intense inner utterance where he dictated her thoughts and actions. There was this hidden feeling, however, that maybe she could have both worlds and would not have to submit to the traditional paradime of a woman's life to which most of her gender would have gladly yielded.

A young beatnik, Victor, who had studied music at Cambridge University became besotted with Grace. He adored her innocent beauty which reminded him of Eve. Victor loved the way she discussed all the arts, in particular, her passion for ballet and her love of reading. So their shared interests created a close intimate relationship. He loved her to the depths of his soul. Grace was unsure. She didn't quite know why. Maybe their difference in social class worried her and of course she knew her father would sneer at his background, even though he was educated. Grace just knew that to be kind, she would have to curtail their relationship for Victor's sake as well as her own. She told him that their relationship would have to remain platonic and Victor was devastated. He could not believe that the girl he cared for so much, could not and would not return his love. There was no more friendship and Victor disappeared into hiding.

Grace was offered a job as an au pair in Hampstead. As a live-in nanny, she would have to leave Peggy and Moira which was upsetting, yet thrilling at the same time. She would be living with a celebrated family in a very large house and of course she felt she would have responsibility for the safety and care of two children. There was Jenny, who was six years old, with auburn ringlets framing her petite elfin face. She loved to be cuddled as her mother, Laura, an actress was often too busy with her theatrical roles. Her father, Brian, was also a very successful actor and had little time to show enough affection to his adorable child. Michael, aged eight, with his dark brown curls, was a mischievous imp who would love to play and tease people. The emotions that Grace felt were so new, and she felt a warmth rise up inside her as the children created a feeling of tenderness that had been lacking all her life. Grace was content in her new role. She was often able to visit her favourite Italian coffee bar and chat with her friends there when the children were at school or in the evenings, when their parents weren't performing. On one of these occasions, Grace was sitting at a table enjoying a coffee and a Chelsea bun, when she was attracted to a striking looking man sitting opposite to her. He was alone and gazing intently at her with a smouldering stare. He looked very serious and there was no sense of joy in his face. His look was inviting and Grace felt herself shudder as he rose from his seat and walked very slowly and determinedly towards her table. Grace's heart was beating, something that she would become very familiar with. He asked quietly, "May I please sit down at your table?" Grace could not reply. She just nodded silently and submissively, as he moved the chair and sat down brusquely beside her. The paths in life have many routes and her future would be changed permanently from this moment.

Peter Kempson was a tall dark-haired architect. His appearance was commanding. He had the look of a military officer, somewhat like Errol Flynn. Grace was fascinated by his self-confident intelligence. His parents had moved from London to Grimsby when Peter was fourteen years old. His father was in shipping and his mother was a dressmaker. As a young boy, Peter loved drawing and continually amazed his teachers with his designs of cars, buildings and lorries. Having gained a scholarship to the University of York to study Architecture, Peter excelled at this subject, achieving a distinction and consequently found himself a job as an architect in Hemel Hempstead in Hertfordshire. For him, everything had to be in order. Peter loved neatness. Beauty and perfection were his ideals. Control was essential, as this enabled him to feel a sense of mastery of his world. The life of Peter Kempson revolved around his producing perfect plans on the pages of this architectural papers. This discipline reigned supreme within his life where he practised self-restraint in all things: harmony, symmetry and classification ruled his actions. When he attended meetings, he was always one step ahead. He had just been to an important conference at his head office in London's Baker Street and had walked the city streets to concentrate his mind. Passing the coffee bar, he saw a waif-like young woman sitting alone at a table. "She's for me," he muttered to himself, smiling inside at the thought of catching her.

Grace was completely overcome by his charm. She was extremely impressed as he told her about his career. He displayed all the credentials that her father had instilled into her; he was clearly the kind of man that Edward would have approved of. This handsome debonair gentleman seemed to really like her and so Grace used all her charm to keep him interested.

They saw each other as often as they could and their relationship was very physical and passionate. In her naivety and innocence, she relished his strength of character, which made her feel safe and secure. This sense of security, she realised, was something she had always yearned for. No criticism. No coldness. When he held her tightly and told her that she belonged to him, she believed that he would cherish and take care of her.

Victor still loved Grace and felt desperately unhappy that she had rejected him. Once more visiting their coffee shop, he helplessly watched her relationship develop with this man who he despised. He continually tried to warn her against marrying Peter. Grace just assumed that Victor was jealous and consequently took no notice of his words. One day when Grace was waiting for Peter, Victor sat down beside her. She wanted him to leave but he insisted on saying one thing to her. Victor uttered in a quiet tone, "Grace, you are a rose about to bloom, but my sweet flower, Peter is not a gardener. I beg of you for your own sake, please, please don't stay with him. He will leave you with nothing but thorns, having plucked your petals bit by bit." With those words he left and that was the last time she ever saw him.

Peter's hold on Grace was very strong and she was powerless to resist. When he proposed to her with a ring at a restaurant, she did not hesitate and agreed to marry him. He insisted on a quiet wedding with just the two of them plus Moira and Peggy as witnesses. Peter decided that they should not invite their parents as this would only cause complications. "You are mine," he said with whispered strength.

Wearing a white flowing dress and fresh white flowers in her hair, Grace resembled an angel on her wedding day. The sunlight peered in through the stained-glass windows of the registry office in Hemel Hempstead and the beam of light created a halo around Grace's blonde curls and as she looked up at Peter, a shadow fell across them both. It was as if she was a ray of starlight in a stormy sky. In the silvery light of the sun, Grace looked radiant and unveiled by any possibility of darkened clouds.

So, Grace glided into marriage in a blissful shroud of happiness, adoring the man who would promise everything that she had ever wanted. She would be married and command the respect of her parents and maybe even her estranged brother would hold her in high regard too. The future was hers and Peter's. She would be twenty-one soon.

Zoshia 9

It was a brief honeymoon, but Zoshia had never felt happier. How fortunate she was to have met Harvey, she thought to herself. Bruges seemed to be the perfect setting for their special time together; a fairytale medieval town, which had been preserved in time with beautiful squares that were surrounded by doll-like houses. They walked through cobbled alleyways framed by brick archways; sat at the edge of the canal watching the milk-white swans swimming leisurely past them; visited the many historic sights and romantically rode in a horse and carriage. Zoshia had never experienced the joys and delights of a holiday, and to be there with Harvey, was more than she could ever have dreamed of. Their world together was as one and this helped Zoshia to dispel her inner pain. Harvey had unlocked her heart and the misery from within seemed to have escaped.

Liverpool in 1950 was still suffering the effects of World War II. The sustained bombing had been heavy because Liverpool was a large port and was a valuable asset. The city centre remained scarred and full of bombsites and large areas of the town had been flattened. There were small dilapidated tenements huddled together all in desperate need of care and attention. Liverpool's heart had been crushed by air raids and many buildings were left damaged beyond any form of repair. Whatever had been left behind through bombing had been disembowelled by fire. Despite this aftermath, there was optimism, and even though there was rationing and poverty, people were determined and hopeful of better times ahead.

Many parts of the outer regions of Liverpool had been left intact and Harvey had bought a house in a smart suburb and he and Zoshia were blissfully happy. He would work hard all day and his new wife took delight in creating recipes for his meal when he returned home. Even though restrictions of rations intensely limited the outcome of her cooking, they were both living each day in the contentment and warmth of their strong mutual love. Zoshia had lived on a lot less in her life and this seemed luxury in comparison.

It was, however, a huge culture shock for Zoshia to arrive in a city that had never actually been invaded by the Germans. Living in the provinces where no one understood the extreme persecution she had been through, Zoshia found great difficulty in relating to other housewives in her neighbourhood. She felt that somehow people blanked the fact that so many Jews had been sent to death camps or had their lives stolen from them while having to run away from persecution. She knew though that Liverpool had been bombed and that those living in the city centre and not in the suburbs had endured much hardship. Zoshia tried to attend coffee mornings so that she could meet and become acquainted with people. On occasions, Zoshia reached points of utter frustration in her mind; it was as if no one understood or sympathised with her disastrous experiences. She felt as if she was boring others with her discourse and therefore began to refuse many of the invitations which she received.

Old feelings of insecurity started to build up inside her as Zoshia began to feel as if she was an outsider once more. She was a foreigner living in a strange city with people who even thought that she, herself, was from Germany. As she was unable to drive, she had to walk at least two miles to the nearest shops or wait for long periods of time for the bus. Sometimes she preferred the wait at the bus stop, because she loved to chat to strangers who seemed to Zoshia, to display a more keen interest in her. She felt that no one really cared about what she had been through and she found this very difficult to bear. Zoshia was very happy in her marriage and this happiness was clearly evident when Harvey arrived home from work with lots of stories to tell her about people and events that had happened that day. Sometimes during the evening, she would answer telephone calls for him, which made her feel more useful and important. If there were no calls, then they would sit and chat or play music together. If he had to go out then Zoshia would sit and read. She did often feel lonely, despite her love for Harvey, as she had no real outlet for her intellect. Harvey would not allow her to work as he felt it was his duty to care and protect her. Reading was a wonderful companion for Zoshia as she waited for her husband to return home so they could be together and she would envelop herself inside the warmth of his love.

With the birth of their first daughter, Victoria Agnes, Zoshia and Harvey felt an ecstasy like no other. Their life felt complete and Victoria was doted on by both her parents. Zoshia's happiness at being a mother was overwhelming yet seemed the most natural thing in the world. So much love poured out from inside her for her new baby that she felt she would burst. Zoshia had never experienced such intense feelings before, yet she embraced them. The sleepless nights and the near exhaustion were nothing after what she had been through previously in her life. Taking wonderful walks with Victoria through the nearby park and connecting with simple pleasures, Zoshia began once more to feel a sense of value. She continued to love and was loved. This was such a foreign feeling for her and she sometimes felt that she was not entitled to such elation. She had always felt guilty for escaping the concentration camps while others perished. Protecting her daughter almost obsessively gave Zoshia a sense of control in case that happiness would be taken away from her. Deep within her being, she felt a profound sense of inferiority, something that was uncontrollable. Even Harvey found it difficult to comprehend Zoshia's feelings of persecution and guilt. "Why have I been allowed to survive?" she would frequently ask him. "Why was I granted so much happiness while so many had been exterminated by the Germans?" Zoshia would add. Although she loved her family, these thoughts plagued her daily.

After eighteen months, Zoshia gave birth to a beautiful dark haired little boy who she named Raymond. She was totally consumed once again with a powerful love for her son. She did not even imagine that she would have so much love to give to another child. Fulfilment penetrated her world at this point and she spent all her time and energy nurturing her beloved infants. Little attention was paid to her own needs and Zoshia was unable to read or play her new piano, a beautiful gift that Harvey had brought for her. Being a mother and wife was all consuming and for a while her inner self-doubt was abated. Though Harvey worked hard and was often called out to attend patients late at night, Zoshia supported him. Victoria and Raymond had made Zoshia's life complete and with Harvey, who worshipped her, she allowed herself to bathe in her happiness.

The pregnancy of her third child, two years later was an extremely difficult one. The heavy weight within her was unbearable and although she was delighted to be expecting another child, she prayed for the time to pass quickly. It was a struggle for her to cope with the other two little toddlers. She felt heavy and worn-down. Once again, the crouching tiger seemed to try and pounce and cause her to feel overwhelmed and anxious. Zoshia felt isolated and though her mother came from Antwerp to help with the children she felt that there was no real emotional support for her. Guilty at feeling this way, Zoshia found it hard to dispel her anguish. Harvey was immersed in his work and was not able to help her. She was so exhausted by the time he came home, that she could not take part in their former evening rituals of music and laughter and she missed this dreadfully.

Zoshia suffered extreme hardship during labour which seemed to last an eternity. This was her punishment for living, she cried to herself. Jacob, her third child, was born at ten pounds two ounces. The doctor was compelled to employ forceps and Zoshia had been physically torn. This experience caused her great distress, resulting in her utter difficulty in bonding with her baby. She was unable to breast-feed him as she had done with the other two children. Zoshia was unmoved by this. She was devoid of any emotion. Numbness was her escape. No pain. Nothing. Emptiness was too strong an emotion for her. She did not feel and could not feel anything. Diagnosed with post-natal depression, she was incapable of really caring for any of her children for several weeks and throughout this period, even with daily help and her mother present, there seemed to be no feeling or affection for her new little son.

After a few weeks, however, Zoshia's depression began to lift. She was so thankful to feel an improvement in her physical and mental wellbeing. Harvey had suggested a mild anti-depressant, just for the short term and this, combined with her husband's understanding, allowed Zoshia the time to heal. As she held Jacob, she started to feel love for him and she knew he was very special to her. He was such an adorable baby who had inherited her blue eyes. When he stared up at her, Zoshia's heart melted. She hugged him tightly and hardly dared to let him go. Jacob had missed valuable time with her and she was definitely going to make it up to him. "I'm so sorry, little one. I love you so much and will never let you go," she repeated incessantly and possessively to her beloved son.

Zoshia now felt that her family was complete, but she was petrified of becoming pregnant once again. Harvey was very understanding when she suggested that they should sleep in separate bedrooms. He knew that his wife had suffered so much recently and so this was agreed upon. It did not mar their relationship but having three children to care for was not easy. Somehow, she coped due to her strong sense of duty and her love for her family. It was physically demanding work looking after her children and managing the household. Zoshia was lucky enough to own a twin tub washing machine. Daily, she would fill the machine with water and wash nappies, and all her family's clothing; shirts for Harvey were particularly difficult. Before she could spin the clothes, they had to be put through a mangle and then the clothes had to be placed into the spin drier. After this Zoshia would drape the clothing on the clothes airier which was hung over the fireplace. All this effort would take hours. Zoshia had always loved to iron but Harvey insisted she should get help, which she was truly grateful for. She enjoyed cooking for her family but still continued to travel a long distance to the shops and carry home heavy bags of food and nourishment for them all. Although worn out, Zoshia made herself cope with all the chores of a dutiful housewife. Sometimes during the night, she would lie awake and ask herself whether she could have had a career in music or used her language skills profitably. She told herself that as a woman she was expected to look after her husband, her children and her home. Zoshia felt very fortunate to have all that she had but her sense of separateness and isolation never left her. She had to accept that her talents were wasted and fought with all her might not allow these thoughts to rule her.

It was with the arrival of Hayden, Harvey's brother that life became more intolerable. He too had trained as a doctor and had continued the practice in Tonypandy in South Wales after Harvey had left for Liverpool. Haydn lived there, happily married to Chya who had borne him four children. He was two years older than Harvey but had married a lot earlier. He loved his family and his children and was very content with his position as a general practitioner with patients who appreciated his excellent capabilities as a doctor. However, he yearned to become a dentist but had suppressed these desires for a long time. Hayden decided that he would go and stay with his brother in Liverpool and enrol at the university to study dentistry. His wife and family were distraught and begged him not to leave. He loved them dearly but knew in his heart that he had to do this or he would regret it for the rest of his life. It would have been too difficult for him to study at home; there would have been no peace and he would have been required to contribute to home life which would affect his studies. No. He would be better off living with Harvey and Zoshia. They would take care of his needs. It did not occur to Hayden to consider how much work it would be for Zoshia, who had three children. He begged Harvey to allow him to stay, knowing full well that he would agree. It was difficult for Harvey to say no to his brother and so Hayden became the fifth member of the household to rely on Zoshia. This would force her to endure endless days and nights working hard to complete all her onerous and wearisome chores.

While the men were out all day it befell Zoshia to continue her housewife's role, without any real time left to herself. Her endless walks to the shops, taking three children with her each time she went, was a mammoth undertaking in itself. Cooking, washing, ironing and caring for her children was completely draining. Whenever she found this exhausting, she would recall her struggle through the French woodland, taking the young orphans to the safety of Switzerland. Although she was much older now and more worn down, Zoshia told herself that she would just have to stoically stick to her routine of domestic drudgery. In the evenings, Harvey and Hayden would sit and discuss the day's events with each other. Zoshia would finish the household duties and fall into her bed exhausted. Stifled and stagnant, she couldn't remember the last time she played the piano or read any literature. Did men not realise just how much physical work a woman with children had to do? While they were out all day, following a career they loved, Zoshia who had abilities, intelligence and talent, felt less than human. If only she could have learnt to drive. Without the freedom this would have given her, she felt utterly debilitated. Harvey had expressly forbidden her to attempt driving because he told her that he believed that she would be unable to master it. Her spirits were sinking rapidly, and she knew that ultimately, she would drown very quickly and would have no form of rescue. She had to escape.

Zoshia was not intending to abandon Harvey permanently but it was necessary for her to leave Liverpool for a while and visit her family. She could no longer live under such difficult circumstances. Whenever the subject of Hayden was discussed, Harvey would lift his arms in despair. "What can I do, Zoshela? I can't just ask him to leave now, can I? He has his studies and I can't ruin his dream of becoming a dentist," Harvey uttered disparagingly. Zoshia felt insulted that her husband neglected to realise the unhappiness she felt in her life. So, when Harvey and Hayden were at work, she rang her mother and asked if she could bring the children for a visit. Zoshia did not tell Zara the whole truth. However, while packing for them all, tears streamed down her face. She knew this was the right move. Perhaps when she returned she would not feel like a foreigner and a slave. Harvey drove them to the airport in Manchester. The children were quiet, and Harvey's face was ashen. Zoshia could not speak as she felt an icy chill cover her whole body.

At the terminal, after Harvey had hugged his children, Zoshia finally spoke directly to him. "I may not return unless Hayden finds alternative accommodation. It's simple. He must go. I will be in touch." Zoshia felt distraught at walking away from the man she loved. However, she did not look back. They were on their way to Antwerp. Although she desperately felt like she should change her mind, she didn't and stepped onto the plane to Belgium, back to her family and her old life where she had been a single woman.

When she arrived at her parents' apartment in Antwerp, she was surprised at how happy she was to see them all – even Hannah who she hugged and kissed with excitement. They all doted on the children who were very thrilled at receiving lots of attention; plenty of presents and delicious cake to eat. This was a holiday for them and Zoshia tried her best to join in with the fun. Inside, however, she felt nothing but pain and guilt at having taken her children away from their father and not being able to confide in her family about her difficulties with Harvey.

While she could, Zoshia allowed herself to rest and consequently began to relax. This enabled her to reflect on her life and the situation she was in. Looking back at her past, she wondered what had happened to that young, spirited, girl who had suffered so much but still had desires and dreams of being a pianist or a linguist. That person had been extinguished. She thought of Robert and the life she might have had with him. Their love was so simple and uncomplicated. How easy it was then. No more dreams. She was chained. Trapped. No choices to be made. Condemned. It was as if she was hidden in the war, but this time a personal one and she felt like curling up into a corner and burying herself forever.

Grace 10

Unrealised and unfulfilled expectations and wishes were destroyed for Grace as Peter revealed very early on in their marriage the true nature of his character. He initially displayed his calculating and controlling personality by insisting that his wife transfer her substantial inheritance from her grandmother to him. He claimed it was her duty as a wife. "It is important that you obey me, Grace, as I am your husband and you are obliged to abide by my wishes," he asserted in a dominating tone.

"Very well," she replied deferentially, "I will attend to it directly," trusting the love between them.

On the 15th April 1953 Grace instructed the bank to transfer the money into Peter's account. This left her penniless and utterly dependant on her husband. Once this transaction had been completed, Peter informed her coldly, "I have only married you because you are perfectly middle class and you have affluent parents." Grace immediately burst into tears, hardly able to believe what she had just been told. She ran to the bedroom her vision blighted by the tears in her eyes. Grace could not contain her sobbing. "Oh, what have I done?" she remonstrated uncontrollably. "What have I done?" Grace was devastated and realised the dreadful mistake she had made.

"Grace, stop that dreadful blubbering at once. Pull yourself together," Peter commanded, as he roughly pulled her by her arm and slapped her callously across her cheeks several times, which stunned her. Following this, Peter proceeded to press his body to hers in a rough and cold manner. She was powerless to escape his advance and weakly submitted to his will.

The liberty of her youth had been imprisoned by error and ignorance which caused Grace to marry such a barbaric brute. She could not reveal her mistake to her father so prematurely in the marriage. Maybe things would get better, she hoped. Perhaps Peter did not really mean those hurtful words he had spoken and she silently succumbed to a future with the man who had forced her to grow up.

Peter informed his wife that they would be having a short honeymoon in Paris. Grace was not sure about his meaning but hoped that this was the turning point and that her husband had changed his mind about their relationship. "By the way," he added flippantly, "my friends Martin and his wife Lydia, are coming with us. I'm sure you won't mind if they accompany us, will you?" Grace bowed her head to hide her disappointment. She did not want Peter to sense how she felt. The view of the floor made her feel like her mother, who always seemed to have her head tilted downwards. "Grace!" he commanded in a dominating voice. She looked up at him and smiled. Acting was second nature to her. She had acted all her life and how was this any different? She saw her father standing in front of her: his face – not Peter's. But Grace tried not to let her thoughts and visions control her imagination or she knew she would be lost.

The party arrived in Paris and as they checked into their small hotel, the rain began to drizzle – rain which represented the dampening of Grace's marriage to her husband. When they had unpacked, Peter suggested that they should go for a walk and see the city. "Let us admire the elegant, refined and sophisticated architecture," he ordered and promptly issued the directive for their tour. As it was early morning they would have plenty of time to look around.

Grace followed her husband and his friends as they walked along the Champs – Éysées towards the Arc de Triomphe. It was an endless trek and Grace found it hard to keep up with them – her tiny legs walking twice as fast because the other three were so tall in comparison to her. Peter acted as though they weren't even together as he guided his friends, pointing out various landmarks. She thought how entirely apart she and her husband were from each other; separated as much as two disenchanted lovers could be.

The grey rain fell onto the River Seine. There was no glimmer of sun to illuminate the water; just a mournful mist hovering. The Arc de Triomphe looked sombre as they observed the Tomb of the Unknown Soldier and the eternal flame burning in front. Grace could not feel any enthusiasm as her loneliness consumed her, wrapping around her like a mantle. Suddenly she experienced severe cramps in her stomach and she desperately searched for a public convenience. Running as fast as she could, Grace eventually hurried past a queue and just in time she managed to find an available public conveience. But there was nothing to clean herself with. Grace looked in her bag. She had no tissues left as these had been used earlier for her tears. Suddenly, she noticed her marriage certificate hidden within her passport. That will be perfect, she thought, and she tore it up into manageable sized pieces. This was all it was worth.

Having emerged outside, Grace saw the trio standing together, laughing and chattering. She smiled to herself believing that the action she had just taken had given her strength to carry on the tour. She dared not complain, as they walked and walked. It seemed like an eternity. At last they stopped for a late lunch in a café. Grace enjoyed this as she was able to observe the various elements of life carrying on around her while her companions talked together barely giving her a thought. "I have paid the bill," Peter stated earnestly. "Grace would you please wait here for a while. We are going for a walk together. Don't go away or we won't be able to find you," he added in a mocking tone. Grace said nothing. She was relieved to see them go. It would enable her to relax and be herself in Paris.

While she sat there, Grace thought about what they had seen through Peter's guidance. She had seen the Eiffel Tower, a large construct of metal pushing through the perpetual skyline. In normal circumstances she might have felt differently. Her husband had insisted that it was essential to visit the Notre Dame Cathedral. Yes, Grace did see its beauty (though she despised religious places). She had especially enjoyed the interior of the building with its kaleidoscopic, glowing, stained-glass windows and the soothing sound of the voices of the choir as they sung mass. Peter had pointed out the exterior carvings of the kings from the Middle Ages. As she had observed the huge edifice, she had been saddened by the lack of the sun's rays to light up the humanity of man's creation. It was, to Grace, a nightmare. Her religious faith had died, and she felt that this building represented the embers of her belief. She saw it as building of dreary oppression which reminded her how her theological ethics had shrunk and withered. She saw Notre Dame as a metaphorical tyrant representing the strict rules and doctrines of her cruel spouse.

Lost in thought, Grace had not noticed how one hour had passed. When the waiter asked if she wanted anything, she declined as she had no money – nothing. Suddenly realising this, a sense of fear overwhelmed her. She had no idea where Peter and his friends had disappeared to. Frightened to remain in the café as there was a queue forming, Grace knew that she couldn't go very far or she would not be found by Peter. Distressed and alone, she sat on the edge of the pavement as tears meandered over her cheeks. She felt so humiliated. This was Paris, the city of love which had been transformed into one of wretchedness and misery. As dusk began to fall, Grace watched the speed of the traffic and the movements of people hurriedly brushing past her with footsteps of intention. In contrast, she was static, motionless like all the monumental buildings. Perhaps, Grace thought, Peter has deliberately left me here and just as she stood to action, to find a policeman, the party returned and she was immediately ushered back to their hotel.

The honeymoon had been a disaster and Grace was relieved to be on the return journey to England. When they arrived back at their house and Peter had driven his friends home, Grace purposefully and deliberately cut up the wedding photographs with her best pair of scissors.

Living in Hemel Hempstead in a respectable three-bedroom house, Grace should have been overjoyed at being comfortably married and settled with a man who was able to provide for her materially. She had become the perfect housewife, which her father had always insisted she should aspire to. Was this it? Was this how it was meant to be? she asked herself.

The disintegration of a young human life was clearly evident to see. She was a woman ensnared. Grace lived her days, weeks, months and years in utter fear and trepidation from which there seemed to be no escape.

She bore Peter two children; Brian and Sean. Grace loved her little boys so much and wanted to protect them from their callous, cold father. Fortunately, while they were so young, Peter did not harm them. However, he continually abused Grace verbally and physically. Living her life in fear and trepidation, Grace unsuccessfully tried to cater to his every need. Often, she would feel herself tremble, especially when his look pierced her with his merciless eyes which seemed to gaze beyond her, yet to Grace, displayed his sadistic intentions towards her. His stare created doubt and fear as he accused her with a serious mockery. His egotism had lain hidden like a serpent under a mound covered with flowers. No one knew of his cruelty and believed him to be a charming and courteous gentleman. He told her that everything she did was unsatisfactory. If she tried to dress to please him, he told her she looked like a tart. "Why don't you try harder?" he would say repeatedly. She realised that this was a bell ringing in her mind which sounded the alarm for the death knell of the drama of their marriage when Peter uttered those words of contempt, "My expectations of you have experienced a great deal of disappointment. You must know that you are worthless and insignificant. Our marriage is valueless and futile and it is all your fault for being so incompetent and ineffectual."

Grace was petrified of his sexual demands. His torture knew no bounds. At the hands of her demonic husband, she suffered painful injuries. It was as if the pleasure he gained from her suffering intensified when she begged him to stop. Grace feared that his cruelty might even kill her. Sometimes she would find it impossible to get out of her bed in the morning as she was in so much pain following her night of abuse and ill-treatment. Looking at her reflection in the mirror, Grace could not even recognise her swollen and disfigured face which stared back at her, with bruised, bulging, black lumps around her eyes which she could barely open. Her head was covered with bald patches that were created when her tormentor dragged her across the floor, with his fists wrapped tightly around her hair. How would she ever escape from him? Who could she tell? What would he do to her if she did? These were questions that prevented Grace from informing anyone. Grace was too ashamed to go for medical help and was embarrassed in case she was asked questions. Too terrified to refuse his demands, Grace had to comply with them. She was living in a nightmare world, ruled by the devil in human form. Each day she would be given little reminders of his dirth of love, the early apparent love which had metamorphosised into torment. Unable to leave him because she had two children to care for, she contacted her parents. "Oh Father," she exclaimed "I need money so that I can take the children away from this cruel monster I have married. He tortures me and hurts me. My eyes are black and blue, and I have a cut lip. Please, please help me."

Edward replied curtly, "Grace, you have made your bed so now lie in it. Goodbye."

In desperation, she rang her brother to ask him why their parents would not help her. George curtly replied, "What do you expect them to do? He is your husband." Both men had hung up on her and the blank sound of the phone, which was left, made her realise how alone in the world she was.

Without contraception, Grace was entirely defenceless and was completely vulnerable to the sexual molestation which Peter dictated. Unprotected, Grace became pregnant again. Peter did not contain his abuse at all. His demands seemed totally unbearable. Fearing for her unborn child, she begged and begged for him to stop. Continually, he would rape her and laughed during her tearful pleas. Beatings continued to be a daily occurrence and he became even more abusive. She could still see that he took extreme pleasure in degrading her despite her being heavily pregnant. Sometimes she would pray to die in childbirth so that her distress would come to an end. Forlorn and alone, Grace could not see a way forward but when she held her children, she realised that she had to survive for them.

Despite her suffering, Grace gave birth to a sweet innocent daughter, who had inherited her mother's blonde curls. Tara gave Grace the love she needed and as she cuddled her baby, she wondered how anyone so evil could have fathered such an angel. Her stay in hospital had been helpful in recreating the vital strength which Grace had lost. When Peter came to visit with the children, she realised that somehow, she would have to try and get away from him. The children had been cared for by Glynis, Peter's cousin. She was a valuable help and the boys seemed happy. Yes, Grace would find a way of recreating a new life for them. She did not envisage how difficult this would be. First, she would try and get back to a routine and not let any cruelty dissuade her from her resolve.

Grace was fortunate. Peter told her that he would be going away for three days and while giving her house-keeping money, he added that she should think about ways of improving her behaviour and attitude. She was relieved that he actually stuck to his word and left her alone with the children. Over the years, she had managed to save some money from her house-keeping allowance, so she used it to contact a lawyer. In shock, Grace could hardly bear to hear his communication to her. He bluntly stated, "In the event of a separation or divorce, your husband would certainly have priority of custody of your children." He spoke this in a very unemotional way and without real sympathy for her plight. As Grace left his office in tears, she gathered up her strength and walked determinedly to the nearest police station. She spoke to a male police officer about the continued assaults which she had suffered. Even after hearing about having been brutally beaten, the police informed her that she would not obtain help from them as it was a marital issue and they could not interfere. How could this be? Grace cried to herself. It seemed that women were treated very unjustly. It seemed that they were considered as second-class citizens.

Without Peter around, and after the children had gone to bed, Grace found time to consider her position. She enjoyed spending time alone and this improved her spirits. Yes, her parents had told her that it was her duty to stand by her husband. Yes, she had no independence, little money and no support. She was an abused young woman with three children. She had to be strong. Somehow there would be a way for her to find a route out of this impossible situation, even though the authorities had virtually told her to grin and bear it. Yes, she was a female. Yes, she had no rights. She asked herself why women were treated as inferior beings. Maybe the time will come in the future when women will be granted equal rights to men, but until then, I will have to take control, she thought positively. Grace had to plan her flight from her husband's ferocity and save the threatened lives of herself, her two little boys and her baby girl.

This choice of certainty would be her weapon to gain freedom.

Zoshia II

Harvey felt distraught. How could he not see what was happening? Zoshia was unable to cope with everything at home. I will have to speak to Haydn directly and persuade him to leave – he thought anxiously. After their supper, which Hayden had made for them, the two brothers sat down together to talk. Harvey hated confrontation and kept postponing his directive to Hayden. He felt anxiety rising in his chest, as he did not want to create tension between them. So just as he was thinking about his reticence, Harvey heard himself utter in a very direct manner, "You will have to find somewhere else to live, I'm afraid. Zoshia is struggling with looking after so many people and now that she is in Antwerp, I'm scared that she may not return. You do understand, don't you Hayden?" Silently Harvey's brother stood up and looked directly into his eyes. The silence seemed to last an eternity.

"I am going upstairs to pack. I will leave tomorrow. I will look for somewhere near to the university and you can pack too. You have an urgent plane to catch to bring your wife and children home," Hayden stated, smiling at his brother and patting him on the back playfully.

Harvey made his way to Antwerp. He was so frightened of losing his beloved Zoshia and their children and he prayed that they would receive him with open arms. As he arrived at the front door and knocked, little Victoria opened the door of the apartment and gave him a big hug. Harvey could feel the tears welling up in his eyes as everyone greeted him warmly. "Come in, Harvey, and have some cake," Zara said in a warm and inviting manner.

As they sat down together, Harvey took Zoshia to one side and told her that Haydn had moved out and that he couldn't wait for them all to come home. Zoshia was ecstatic that Haydn had left because it showed her that Harvey had put her first. "Please come home with me Zoshela. You are my life," he pleaded with longing in his voice.

"Of course, I will come back. We are one and with our children, our love will carry us through any more hardships that we may have to endure," she replied with so much sincerity in her voice that Harvey felt himself shiver.

Zara, Smule and Hannah were happy that Harvey agreed to stay a while and for the next couple of days they all laughed and joked together in an embracing family cocoon. Zara was pleased that her daughter's engaging smile had returned. Zoshia was happy once more and that was all that mattered. Saddened that their daughter would be returning to England, Smule and Zara reminded her how strong she really was and that they loved her. Zoshia had never experienced such obviously open affection and was extremely uplifted by it. Her parents were aging and had never recovered from their wartime hardship. She looked at them: two elderly people, bearing the physical and mental damage from their war experiences and she shuddered. Leaving them would be difficult now. She did not realise that this would be the last time she would see them.

Harvey and Zoshia and their children returned to England a couple of days later and their former happiness was restored. Life did not seem so unbearable and it was during this period that Zoshia learned to drive. Each time she took her driving test, she failed. "This is the hardest thing I have ever tried to do," she moaned. It was after the fourth attempt that she eventually passed the test. Harvey was hesitantly pleased for her even though he knew that she wasn't a particularly good driver. Zoshia seemed to park the car some distance from the kerb and never worried about cars who drove behind her. "My instructor told me not to worry about the cars behind, only those in front of me," she retorted whenever anyone criticised her driving. Now she had more freedom and at last could drive herself to the shops for the daily provisions.

As time passed and the children grew older, Zoshia and Harvey enjoyed their life together. Sometimes they would drive a few yards away from their children walking home from school. Victoria was now ten years old and she held the hands of her two little brothers in a very domineering way. Harvey and Zoshia would laugh at their offspring and talk about how lucky they were to have a family they could cherish.

It seemed as if nothing could come between them. However, life, can find a way of altering things in an instant.

Was it providence? Was it destiny? Harvey beckoned to his wife one morning to sit down, as he had something to tell her. Zoshia could see by the position of his head which was turned away from her, that this was serious. "Zoshia," his voice muttered in a loud silent tone. "I have been told that I have bladder cancer. I knew! I knew! There was blood. I ignored it. I knew…" he said faltering in his words as he struggled to communicate the disastrous information. "I did not want to confront the issue but when I finally went for a test, my worst fears were realised." Silence. Stillness. No words were uttered. Zoshia was dumbfounded. Her beloved Harvey. How would he cope? Her children. How would she be able to tell them?

She would cope. In her state of complete shock, Zoshia remembered how she and Hannah had managed to bury her beloved parents when she returned to Antwerp two months previously. Zoshia knew that from then on she would have to be strong for herself and her sister. How she would miss her parents, she thought. Even though they had lived in separate countries, Zoshia had known they were there if she needed them. How could they have died within two days of each other? It was as though neither one could live without the other… "Zoshia! Aren't you going to say anything? Zoshia, oh Zoshia!" His wife could not believe that death confronted her again like an old acquaintance: it was both familiar and completely surreal. She was stunned by the ache of inevitable destruction.

As Harvey brought her back to reality, Zoshia replied, "I will help you. We will battle this together. I am just like my father. I am strong." Harvey held her close knowing that he could rely on this caring and compassionate woman who he loved so much. Zoshia knew that from now on their lives would be controlled by the disintegration of her adoring husband. She had spent the most part of her life fighting battles but he had been cossetted in comparison. A gentle soul, she would have to take charge of him and make sure that her family were protected from the hurt that this would cause. She must not give up for the sake of her husband and her children.

Year after year, Zoshia spent a large part of her time travelling to and from the hospital to visit Harvey. In moments of remission he would be sent home and could see his children, who seemed to have become teenagers without him even noticing. Although there were some savings and their home was not mortgaged, Zoshia had to work hard to organise the household accounts. Harvey gave up his medical practice which resulted in a small income from his medical superannuation contributions. Zoshia paid for a home help because of the frequent visits to her suffering husband at the hospital. Somehow, she found the strength to support him, even though she saw her life destroyed through watching him deteriorate into a shadow of his former self. Zoshia hardly recognised this old, withered, grey haired man except for his intense green eyes which told her of his love for her in the midst of the unbearable pain he was suffering.

Harvey eventually passed away at just after midnight on the 1st January 1968 – Zoshia's birthday. What cruel hand of fate would allow this to happen? This was a powerful blow to her, but she knew that her precious husband was at peace at last. Zoshia realised that love and death were two sides of the same coin. This gave her a kind of relief, though she was unable to externalise her grief, focussing now on her children and their sadness. She loved Harvey so much and could not bear to lose him. How could she live without the man who had meant everything to her.

After the funeral, Zoshia collapsed. She had felt the room turn and spin around as everyone was eating sandwiches, drinking tea and generally chatting. She wandered how people could just talk in a normal manner, when her husband had gone – had left her alone. She woke up in a hospital bed surrounded by her children and her sister. Zoshia had been given tranquilisers to calm her and she left hospital feeling much better. Hannah had been very supportive which helped Zoshia to relax. She had arrived with her husband a week before Harvey's death. On returning home, Zoshia found it difficult to physically and mentally cope with her grief. Hannah was helpful in organising the household chores and did her best to comfort the family. She had married late in life in Antwerp to Maxim Martor, a kind man who doted on his wife. This had made her a much more caring person and she adored her sister's children. She loved to put her arms round them and comfort them when they showed sadness at their father's death. Hayden returned to comfort the family but did not stay long, as he was not able to grapple with his brother's family's misery.

Zoshia wandered how she would be able to carry on. The first step was to sort out Harvey's clothes. He had possessed a huge, brown, oak wardrobe which contained his life's possessions. Although he had not been a materialistic man, he loved to dress smartly: always insisting on wearing a shirt and tie. When Zoshia opened the central mirrored door of his wardrobe, she at once felt her dizziness return. How often had she carefully hung up his shirts and tidied his suits? Her fingers shakily stroked the clothing. The majesty of this wardrobe had always ruled the bedroom. Each section of its compartments represented the purgatory she was in now and the paradise of the memory of her beloved Harvey. As she picked up his black spectacles, she could see his emerald eyes telling her that everything would be alright. When she discovered his stethoscope, Zoshia could no longer carry on the search and everything would need to remain in the wardrobe for a while longer. The charity would have to wait until she was ready.

Zoshia appreciated all the help she received but she knew that ultimately it was she who would have to take control of her life if they were all to survive intact. She received yet another blow when her solicitor told her that Harvey had not taken out life insurance. How would she exist with three children to care for? A small widow's pension was paid to her but this payment was meagre for all their needs. Zoshia's only consolation was that the house was not mortgaged. As her strength slowly returned, plans were formulated. Her resolve to make life bearable for her family was her primary motive for living. She would spit at death and make life work for them. Zoshia braced herself for a future without the man she loved and as a lone parent fighting for survival.

Grace 12

Freedom for Grace was her constant need. This word, Grace held dearly within her unhappy heart. She was tied closely to the devil and was unable to set herself free from her chains. Divorce was a man's prerogative. Grace could not secure a divorce as Peter held the purse strings. It was a desperate situation, as she knew that it would be impossible for her to cope alone financially with her children. At the very least, he did provide for them.

It was September 1968. The family moved to Warwick, as Peter had acquired a new position running a firm of architects in that area. It was a comfortable home and materially Grace wanted for nothing. She frequently wondered how she could earn her own money. The answer came to her. Sewing. As an excellent machinist, Grace performed alterations for people's clothes initially and eventually progressed to dressmaking. She became very much sought after and this enabled Grace to secretly save her earnings, as she never dared to tell her husband that she was paid for her endeavours.

It had become very clear to Grace that Peter had very strong mental problems and a personal inferiority complex which made him so uncontrollable and unreasonable. She began to realise that she was not responsible for his furious, unhealthy behaviour towards her. Even so, Grace lived her life in constant fear of his intimidation and emotional cruelty. "You are worthless," he repeatedly told her, clearly enjoying her tears and pleas. What could she do? In these moments she felt helpless, and could not envisage any way out for fear of losing the custody of her children. So, silently, she suffered. When these incidents were over, Grace felt she was compensated by the fact that Peter would often disappear for long periods of time; sometimes days; sometimes for weeks on end. What Grace didn't know was that he was secretly deceiving her with another woman. When he would return, Grace had to endure his persistent verbal abuse and further physical injuries which he would inflict on her. This abuse continued for several years. He always gave her a meagre housekeeping allowance for her and the children and kept any capital for himself. There was very little money but she did have a home. She would constantly pray for one of his long absences. It was only then, without the callous and cruel monster torturing her day after day, that Grace found a form of peace. Living with her family, without her torturer, gave Grace a sense of emancipation, despite the fact that she suffered extreme hardship financially.

Eventually, Peter moved in with his mistress and so was frequently away from the house. He would occasionally visit and in these dreaded moments he virtually ignored Grace in his efforts to make her feel unworthy. She was oblivious to this and was utterly grateful that he did not physically attack her. Housekeeping money was paid into her bank account and together with her nimble sewing skills, Grace managed to survive and cater for her children's needs. It was important to her to take control of her situation and Grace was relieved that Peter paid the mortgage.

On one afternoon, during one of his visits and to Grace's extreme surprise, Peter informed Grace that he wanted to divorce her. "You have given me no choice. You have made my married life unbearable with your constant wingeing and moaning. You are nothing to me and so I am leaving you and ultimately, we will be divorced. I will share the proceedings of the sale of this property with you, so that you may find somewhere to live," Peter stated to her with an icy coldness. He wanted to make her cry for the last time. She was completely mute. She wanted to scream. She wanted to shout with rapture. She said nothing. When he left, she laughed and cried together hysterically. Grace was in a state of delirium. At last she was rid of the demon who she now cursed, even though he was the father of her children. Her delight was also tinged with anger – anger towards the male sex. Grace vowed never, ever would she trust any man. There was only one person who could be relied on – herself.

When the initial relief subsided, she became anxious at having to move house. She did not want to argue about wanting to stay in the marital home because she was happy that Peter gave her custody of the children, so that he would be free to live his own life. Grace did not want to rock the boat. Something had to be done so that she could have complete financial independence. After much research, she enrolled in a part-time teaching course. Grace obtained a small grant from the local authority and started training. It was difficult, but while the children were in school, she could study and when they returned, Grace was a mother who cooked and cleaned for them. She was living two roles, a mother and provider. At last she felt free. This liberty to make her own choices was elating, despite the hard work and difficulties which life threw at her. No more physical torture. No more criticism. Grace was moving forwards.

Some mornings were spent at the local library studying for her exams. She found it difficult but loved the practical sessions teaching art at the local school. It was often just a joy to read alone in the libary, surrounded by other people and have a sense of her own singularity. A feeling of being worthy had lifted her confidence as she began to show her talent for teaching. Sometimes, Grace would paint pictures during her teaching practice and the children would adore these sessions.

It was during one of her visits to the library that she accidentally bumped into a young man who seemed to be looking for books in the same section where she was browsing. They laughed and began a whispered chat amongst the novels which surrounded them as if the books were written witnesses to their first meeting.

"Should we go and grab a coffee around the corner?" the softly spoken man asked.

Grace replied, somewhat enthusiastically and to her surprise, "Yes. Sure. I would like that." It can't do any harm, she thought silently to herself and he seems very sweet and friendly.

Michael Portnoy was a lecturer in classics. He was unmarried and lived in an apartment locally. He loved his job and chatted to Grace about his subject which was fascinating for her as she adored classical literature; Greek myths in particular. They formed a friendship very easily.

Each time they met, their relationship seemed to develop romantically. Grace, who was reticent at first, began to relax and allow her inner feelings of fear to be buried, as she started to deeply care for this young, loving man. He made her feel completely at ease and she could be her true self. This was unusual, as Peter had always expected her to behave in a certain way, his way. Michael was overwhelmed by his intense fondness of this beautiful woman with cornflower blue eyes and her enticing smile. He would regularly visit Grace's home and became well acquainted with her children. They liked this friendly person who was clearly close to their mother and would look forward to the days when he came to stay. Eventually Michael moved in and for a while they all settled into family life. Grace was very happy but felt frightened that this contentment would only be temporary.

It took some time before Peter and Grace's property was sold. The fear of where they would go next resurfaced as soon as an offer was placed on their house. Financially this would be difficult for her, but she was resolute and determined to make it work. A surprising support to her problem came from her kind, affectionate Michael. He suggested to her one day, "Why don't we buy a small cottage together? You have enough money for a down payment and I will repay the mortgage."

"Oh Michael," Grace replied, with disbelief yet could not contain her enthusiasm. "I can't believe it. Are you absolutely sure?" She pleaded, wanting complete reassurance, "Are you certain that you want to live with a woman and her three children? Are you sure?" Grace repeated anxiously. Although she would lose her independence, she knew that Michael was sincere and kind and would help to support her and the children.

"I really do care for you all," he responded with a warm and sincere tone to his voice. "We will be one happy family," Michael added enthusiastically, like a young child being given a bag of sweets. Michael seemed so elated and earnest in his idea that Grace agreed. Plans were made and Michael was true to his word. He persuaded Grace to apply for a job as an art teacher and he also found a small cottage for them to live in. It was big enough for all of them. The boys would share one bedroom; Tara would have the other room and they would be able to share. Grace kept pinching herself. Could this be happiness at last?

"It's so lovely here, Michael. I cannot believe this is ours," Grace whispered to him as they surveyed their home. They loved the garden which extended far beyond anything they could have imagined. The veridian lawn was framed with water-coloured flowers and pink blossom that clothed the trees, and radiated a soft colouring, as if their colour and texture had been born from nature's power: the loving soil, the life force of the sun and the replenishing rainwater. The scent within the garden diffused around Grace and Michael in the warming breeze. As they surveyed the scene with happiness, a small shiver crossed Grace's shoulders. Was anyone allowed this much joy? Portraying the essence of her being, her turquoise eyes looked to the heavens and molten tears streamed down her cheeks, splashing onto her finger tips which held Michael's hand close to her heart as the salt water sealed their pledge for the future.

Three days passed and everything was organised in the house. Grace would start her job the following month. She was very excited. However, the fleeting ecstasy which she had experienced with Michael as they moved into their home was suddenly ripped from her. Michael left. He had left her after having shared their lives for just a week. There was no explanation. He had completely disappeared and she was unable to contact him. Grace was devastated. The heartbreak she felt was unbearable. How did she have no idea? Why didn't he speak to her? She cried alone. She thought to herself that it had all been too good to be true. What man would like to take on another man's three children? The boys were now young teenagers and could be very difficult. She felt worthless and not deserving of love. Her heartbreak was exacerbated by the realisation she would have to carry the burden of sustaining her home by herself, by paying the mortgage and all the bills. She had to find a way to bury the pain, as she had done so many times before. Grace convinced herself with all the inner strength she could find that she would manage. She had to.

Zoshia 13

In contemplating her life after Harvey's death, Zoshia realised that no one could have ever predicted the extraordinary alteration in her circumstances. The young women who had left Antwerp with hope and enthusiasm had disappeared. Alone with three children and having to care for them as a single parent was tormenting her mind in ways that she could never have imagined. She hoped to grow old with her husband but this had been snatched away from her. Zoshia's health began to deteriorate rapidly and she developed an abnormal heartbeat for which she took medication.

She told herself that there was no use worrying and dwelling on the situation. It was time to take action. She had to work to earn a living and so Zoshia bravely obtained a job selling massage equipment. Her children were older now and she did not have to look after them in the same way as when they were younger. Although she was not well paid, she managed the job extremely successfully and sold many items to her needy clients through her warm charm. The commission which she earned helped her to support her family. Things seemed to take an upturn and the success of her children at school gave Zoshia much satisfaction and pleasure. Hannah would visit for several weeks at a time as her husband had passed away too. Despite their differences, the sisters enjoyed each other's company and Zoshia also received some financial support from Hannah, as she had been left very comfortable financially by Maxim. Even though her sense of pride made her uncomfortable, she appreciated the help.

Zoshia decided to study languages at an advanced level. She attended evening classes after working during the daytime. Her eldest daughter, Victoria, had left home in order to study art at a Midlands university. She was far away from Zoshia and her mother missed her dreadfully. However, she was happy that Victoria was following her passion. "Good luck my babela," she had cried as Victoria left on the train. She felt a great affinity with her first born as they were both pursuing further education at the same time.

Zoshia passed her Advanced Level examinations and secured a place to study French and German at Liverpool University. At this point in her life she felt very contented. Finding others to study with and discussing issues with lecturers fed Zoshia's mind, which had been stagnant for so long. Zoshia was now swimming without a life jacket and she loved it. Developing a broader outlook on life enabled her to see the world differently. She viewed herself as an independent woman providing for her family. The important thing now was to make sure that her children were successful no matter what it took. This would incur hard work in order to ensure a positive outcome.

It was 1973 and Zoshia's two sons attended university in Liverpool and she opened a language school, having qualified as a teacher. This was because her degree in languages and her teaching qualifications gave her the confidence to do this. Although Zoshia was the sole teacher, she travelled to many different factories to instruct the workers in basic conversational French. The factories were expanding and connecting with Europe and executives benefited from her technical language skills. In the evening she taught German and French to adults, which enabled her to support her children at university.

Although she enjoyed her daily routine, it was nevertheless a lonely time for Zoshia. Her children were studying at university and led their own lives. She yearned for companionship but somehow friendship seemed to elude her. Her tireless working, day and night, prevented her from making friends and socialising within her community where women did not work, but were supported by their husbands. Couples did not invite single or widowed women to their social events. Yes, she was alone. A foreigner. There seemed no real way forward in Zoshia's mind for her to feel a sense of belonging.

Zoshia continued to struggle financially and argued with bank managers; council officials; in fact, anyone who demanded payment from her. She fought to survive, as if her life and the lives of her children depended on it. Zoshia immensely enjoyed teaching adults in evening classes. This gave her a strong personal satisfaction as she was helping people. Also, the opportunity arose for her to develop a close friendship with a male lecturer Ewan Rees. He taught languages as well and this created a connection and a common interest. Ewan would visit her in the evenings when they weren't working and they would converse late into the night. This relationship curbed Zoshia's loneliness and gave her the comfort which she so desperately needed. She had at last found a soul mate on her intellectual level with whom she could engage in deep discussion. She felt less alone having Ewan for a friend. There was no romance between them, just an intense, deep platonic attachment and their ripening friendship blossomed. Life was hard work, as Zoshia felt she was just battling for her very existence; not against a Nazi invasion but a war of her own; a war of survival for herself and her family. Her relationship with Ewan eased the burden, as he made her realise the important job she was doing.

Zoshia was ecstatic when Victoria obtained a position as an art teacher in the Midlands. Her daughter had become self-sufficient and would no longer be a dependant. Her mother was so pleased and proud, despite the fact that she missed Victoria so dreadfully. Zoshia still had the support of her two sons, if not financially but emotionally. It was difficult for them to see their mother work so hard. She saw her workday life as a measure of her independence; she was highly respected and her opinions mattered. She was no longer the young restricted woman. The former had been replaced by a wise, mature middle-aged adult despite her unquestionable inner sense of despair which she constantly tried to suppress. On a personal level, the feelings of an unfulfilled life would often completely overwhelm her, as Zoshia continued to support herself and her sons. It was difficult for her to bury the feeling that her early musical talent, which had shown so much promise, had amounted to nothing. Materially, the hopes and dreams of a secure life had been thwarted. Zoshia would continue to ask why. Providence? Had this life been pre-destined? Still believing in her religion she felt a sense of betrayal in thinking this. Zoshia believed that her cup of life had not really been filled. Somehow it had always seemed to be empty, as the torments that she had experienced had sucked the life from her cup and destroyed it sip by sip. Although she longed to be cared for once more, both emotionally and financially, Zoshia knew that this would never happen. Having been loved by Harvey had given her strength to continue life without him. The enormity of her love for her children had endowed her with greater courage than ever before. Of course, she now had the credentials to allow her to earn a living despite her loneliness. Her work would be her salvation and she would have to be grateful.

Grace 14

Grace begged for some financial help from her father. When he refused, she asked her brother for support but he too declined to come to her aid. Somehow, Grace managed to maintain the mortgage repayments from her teaching salary and with emotional help from her friends at school, she began to see a way forward. Luckily, Michael had given her his part ownership in the cottage and this encouraged Grace to feel independent and thankful. She realised the importance of freedom to make her own choices and decisions. If she failed, it would be her fault and she would recognise this herself, without having to be abused and criticised by her father, brother or husband. It was as if she had finally escaped from the tyranny of male domination. In some sense it was a delight to make mistakes and correct them herself.

After the betrayal by Peter and Michael, Grace found it difficult trusting others. Although she had a number of close friends, who she relied for support, she knew that she would never be able to trust a man again. Her pain prevented this. Grace was very popular in the academic environment of school and she was a complete breath of fresh air. Loved by the children she taught, she had the gift of making each one of them feel special. In reality she did not allow her outer shell to be penetrated to reveal the despair within.

As a successful teacher, Grace flourished and she developed a close friendship with a much younger female teacher who worked in the same school in Warwick. Comfort was found in their deep discussions about life, art and literature. They valued each other's friendship which would last a lifetime.

Both women adored the arts and together they would visit galleries, participate in painting and drawing classes, and attend the theatre. This was a distraction for Grace from the devastation of her loss of Michael. She had found it difficult and lonely without him. Although her colleagues at school were supportive and positive, it was difficult for her to disclose her suppressed emotions. Now that she had found a trustworthy companion , Grace was able to impart all her feelings to her; things she had never revealed to anyone. Crying involuntarily, she related the distress she had experienced during the ordeal of her tormented marriage. Grace did not talk about Michael too much as her feelings were still raw. So with the emotional support of her friend and the enjoyment of their pursuit of the arts together, she felt an improved sense of her artistic identity.

It was with great excitement that Grace and her friend decided to take a few days holiday abroad to enjoy some sunshine and take delight in the Greek culture. Grace arranged for another friend to take care of her children. She desperately wanted to escape to somewhere different and forget her life and Michael, just for a short while. It was a cheap holiday and they stayed in a small apartment by the sea in Agios Nikolaos, Crete. This was a coastal town which nestled beside the gulf of Mirabello; a little haven of beauty.

The two friends enjoyed sunbathing and swimming in the sea. The golden beach with soft warm sand allowed Grace to relax. Feeling the grains caress her arms and legs as she lay there gazing up at the sun, she dared her eyes to remain open, while the yellow rays penetrated her soul. At the same time Grace could smell the essence of the seaweed which was so serene that it seemed like a mystical experience. Her spirits had been lifted as she looked at her companion and thanked her.

Together, they sat in the afternoons, drinking tea and eating cake by the lagoon. Grace informed her friend that it was told that the goddess Athena had bathed in the lake. How pleasant and relaxing it was to watch the glittering sun sparkling like a jewel on the clear water.

After their afternoon delights at the taverna, the two friends would search the craft shops and buy tiny statues as mementoes of their holiday. Grace had not felt so happy for a long time as she immersed herself in the Greek sculptures and artefacts. Her favourite was a white carved figurine of Botticelli's Birth of Venus; the first powerful woman, Grace thought to herself. She also purchased a petite statue of Aphrodite. These little artefacts would be a reminder of the brief moments spent together with her dearest friend, sharing their interests and their love of art.

They visited the Palace of Knossos which had been destroyed by fire in 1700BCE. They learned about The Minotaur, the monster child who thrived on human sacrifice. Grace shuddered at this tale, realising the potential of her own human sacrifice at the hands of her cruel husband and how she had wondered through the mazes of her married life in fear and desperation. Now she was unchained and as her genuine self she bought a souvenir picture which she would keep to remind her of this visit.

The island of Spinalonga was extremely beautiful. It had been a leper colony, and the barren landscape had become a refuge to isolated people because of this dreadful condition. When Grace and her friend visited, they were overwhelmed by the mysterious, etherial quality of the scenery which was surrounded by the crystal aquamarine sea. Grace pondered the beauty yet could not help but question how many weeping tears had been shed by the poor lost souls who had lived there. There were no souvenirs to be bought, just the fascinating images of the island's enchantment, and the history of its sorrow. As they returned to the mainland, having left the island, Grace looked at the movement of the water and felt a deep sadness. It was as if the ebb and flow of human misery was represented here. Grace would never forget this holiday as it had revitalised her. In friendship the two women returned to England with suitcases packed with memories of their artistic visit to Crete.

Expressing her creative needs was a life force for Grace, as she had always been made to curtail them. In the course of time she became stronger and more confident and eventually allowed herself to have romantic encounters. Her relationships with men were never serious until she met Larry Long, a lecturer at Warwick University. Grace was introduced to Larry at a party held by a school colleague; they were magnetically drawn to each other – an instant, mutual attraction. From that evening they became close, despite meeting just twice a week. Grace felt deliriously happy and allowed herself to fall in love with this handsome artist who had swept her off her feet. She was completely taken in by him, but he told her upfront that he was unhappily married, and this was further complicated by the revelation that his wife was an invalid. His situation made Grace wary of Larry and she knew that developing a relationship with him was very risky. Despite declaring his love for her very quickly, she knew Larry would never leave his wife. Part of Grace felt ashamed at the role she played in Larry's betrayal, but their connection was so deep and out of her control. Their relationship was passionate – Grace had never experienced such ecstasy before. He had become like a drug to her and she adored the addiction. She was unable to tell her children about this relationship, as she felt some embarrassment because they had seen how unhappy she was when Michael had left. Her children had grown up and led their own lives and therefore she felt justified in her closeness with this new, romantic companion. He was so attentive when he was with her. Art was his passion and he shared this enthusiasm with Grace. Convincing herself that what she was doing was right, she told her close friend that a relationship like this would protect her independence, so that she could still lead her own life.

Larry was a painter and exhibited his work. He took Grace to see his paintings and described each of them in turn. He relished the idea of abstracting the human body. Some were minimalised into curved linear lines using shades of one colour. In others, he would select tonal and spacial forms from the naked torso and translate them into overlapping, soft constructions. He would constantly talk about his paintings with Grace and valued her opinion. Grace was forthright in her constructive criticism. She told him that his paintings seemed to be cold and did not display the warmth of humanity. The shapes he produced were interesting but to her, they didn't seem to represent the human figure. Larry dismissed her comments as those of ignorance. Grace tried to discuss her figurative paintings with him but Larry did not show much interest in them. She had no support from him whenever she suggested exhibiting them. This was difficult for Grace because even though she had a professional career, she wanted her personal talent for art to be acknowledged. Always trying to create in the evenings and at weekends, Grace had accumulated a vast number of paintings of landscapes, portraits and some imaginative pieces based on the books she had read. While she was producing her artistic compositions, she felt alive. It was as if her whole being had been taken over and she could forget the blemishes of her past. It would be so exciting for her to have an exhibition like Larry, but she realised it was merely a futile dream, a dream which would never happen. She knew he would not support her in this. It was a man's world and she would have to bear it. Grace would suppress these dreams because survival was imperative. It was essential for her to concentrate on her job and maintain her finances in order to pay the mortgage. Larry could achieve his dreams which he seemed to take for granted and she could enjoy him for now. For Grace, love would have to be snatched in between pain and loss. She told herself that she was stealing something back from life and hoped she would not be punished. Love was very important to her; it was the sunlight of the soul. For Grace, life was love. She knew that Peter had made her hate herself and she would never ever forget her suffering. Larry was not like Peter, he was warm and affectionate even though he was very self-centred. Their meetings were sporadic and he was often unreliable in his arrangements with her; sometimes he might not appear for several weeks. But it was the same routine: Grace would continually forgive him after he implored her to allow him to return. She adored Larry and could no longer envisage her life without him.

Zoshia 15

The lack of money which Zoshia suffered had dictated her lifestyle; she worked to drown her loneliness, despite her sons still living at home. She lived as a foreigner in a city of people who did not understand her. Ewan Rees had moved to another part of the country and so that friendship no longer gave Zoshia the comfort she craved. Once she had been married to a doctor and lived comfortably with him and their children. Now she had become elderly and those children had become independent from her as young adults. Who needed her now? Hannah was still living in Antwerp but she was not a well woman and Zoshia did not see her often. She too was alone, but was financially secure and continued to offer her sister support. Zoshia appreciated this, but life was still difficult.

Never having been able to overcome her intense feelings of paranoia created by her experience during the Holocaust, every day was endured rather than enjoyed. Zoshia would wake with her heart beating rapidly in case she would have to quickly run away from her home. There was the sense of fear that somehow, she would be discovered and consequently imprisoned. No, she had not experienced the gas chambers. Her story was not as dreadful. But she had suffered like many other Jews at escaping that monstrous cruelty which would have ultimately ended in torture and unbearable death. The guilt at surviving had never left her and it seemed now that no one really cared about her abysmal life during the war and her family's personal holocaust.

Zoshia often felt herself drowning in her memories of the darkness of the Nazi persecution. Although she knew that she had been brave in her youth and had contributed greatly to the welfare of Jewish children, it was as if this was just a horrific memory. She knew that her younger self had not just submitted to life but had made an impact on it. Who could she talk to about it now? Who would ever know the story of her life? Zoshia felt that no one would care about her experiences as she was not in an extermination camp and therefore did not suffer in the same way. The feelings of apparent rejection were heartbreaking for her. She did not want rewards or any acclaim for the part she played. She just wanted mere acknowledgment. Unable to confide her true inner feelings to her children because they would be upset, Zoshia attempted to curtail her torment and focus on her teaching and the happiness of her family.

Zoshia was delighted when her eldest son Raymond married Laura. At last her beloved boy had found a sweet, gentle girl who would love him in a way that he had been used to. They were very compatible, and she had every confidence in the marriage. Raymond had qualified as an optician and was about to open his own shop. She could certainly feel successful in her role as a mother and bathed in the glory of his achievement.

It was not long afterwards that Zoshia's younger son, Jacob, qualified as a lawyer. It had been a struggle finding the money to finance his studies but his qualification was the ultimate dream for her third child who had caused her so much physical pain at his birth. She loved him so much and the triumph she felt when seeing his practising certificate knew no bounds. Shortly after this tremendous accomplishment, he married a young girl, Belinda who it was clear to see, adored him. With both sons married, Zoshia prayed that their lives would be filled with health and happiness and that they would experience a joyful and secure marriage without the struggle that she had encountered. Although her sons had married late in life, having focused on their careers, their happiness gave her a great sense of relief. She prayed the burden of suffering and trauma would not pass on to the next generation and they would live life completely.

Family life had ceased for Zoshia who now lived alone. She questioned the path that her life had taken from childhood to the elderly woman she had become. The dreams she had of utilising her musical talents as a pianist were never realised. Zoshia remembered how Harvey had loved her piano playing and the evenings they had spent together playing Chopin. In her mind she heard Gunther's voice shouting loudly at her for making an error. Zoshia could hear him telling her that she would be a concert pianist if she took note of his directions. Her ambitions were firstly thwarted by the war and then slowly diminished by the household burden to which a woman had to succumb. This depressive outlook, despite her children's successes, reflected her disappointment in her personal creative failure and this belief combined with her extreme loneliness took its toll. No one was aware of her own isolation and Zoshia could see no real way forward to personal contentment.

It was 1990. Health issues demanded that she should retire. The death of Hannah dealt her an enormous blow that shook her to the core. All her life she had tried to escape from the presence of her dominating sister but now that she was no longer alive, Zoshia found her loss unbearable. Hannah had been the last person of her generation to understand what they had been through and suffered during the war and now she was gone. Zoshia had been left some money by Hannah which enabled her to feel the financial security she had craved all her life but this could not replace the loss of her only sibling.

Life has a way of altering things. Just as Zoshia thought she was doomed to years of loneliness and sadness, Victoria, told her that she might return home in the near future. She was not sure when, as this depended on her being able to transfer her job to Liverpool, but she was contemplating the idea. She had loved her teaching position and her friends but missed Zoshia too much and was making plans to return to her. The excitement which Zoshia felt was an unfamiliar but revitalising feeling that helped dull the pain of her recent bereavement. "She is coming home," she whispered to herself and allowed a small smile to envelop her face. I just hope she doesn't change her mind, Zoshia thought. What if she could not transfer her job? Zoshia would have to face her days completely alone. With this doubt, her happiness submerged into a sea of anxiety. She would not let herself be consumed with thoughts of Victoria's return, knowing that life had never been on her side.

Grace 16

Growing older did not trouble Grace. Despite being middle aged, she was not unduly worried when she saw the wrinkles, which represented her life, embedded in her face, as she glared into the mirror to apply her lipstick. Her watery eyes still exuded the intense blue of her youth and her whitened hair displayed an apparent sagely wisdom, though Grace knew that this was not true. She was content to live in her home and see her friends. She missed her family who lived far away which made visits very difficult. Her brother was in contact from time to time but did not provide any emotional support. Grace often wondered what it must be like to feel truly loved by a man in an unselfish and caring way. The men in her life had used her for their own desires and she regretted the intense influence that her father always had over her which seemed to dictate her choice of male partner and imprisoned the growing woman.

With hard work and determination, Grace's three

children became successful adults and despite the difficulties of their childhood, she was pleased that she had been able to support them through their education and into careers. Brian, Grace's eldest son was a banker and became very successful. He married Angela and she cared for him with a strong belief in his ability to succeed. Sean used his practical skills to develop a thriving building company and led a comfortable life with his wife Lyndsay. Grace's youngest child, Tara, worked very hard to become a caring and hardworking midwife. She lived fairly near to her mother with her husband, Mark, which was a great comfort, as mother and daughter were extremely close.

At this point Grace felt that she had completed her role as a mother and family provider and she embraced the love that she felt for Larry.

As she continued her role as an art teacher and grew even closer to Larry, Grace felt a form of peace at last. Contentment consumed her being and she felt that she would be allowed to live her life uninhibited. Yet again, this serenity was fleeting. In an instant, Larry stopped visiting without warning. He told her that she was entrenched in his being, but this must have been a lie if he was able to abandon their relationship so abruptly. She knew that his wife's illness had worsened and she would need taking care of in a way that she hadn't before. Now she was alone, her world was desolate. Yet again she felt betrayed. This would be the last time. Never, ever again would she allow herself to be emotionally battered. She had told herself this so many times before, but this time she was resolute. For weeks she felt stunned. How could she have allowed herself to be used, sexually and psychologically? She had taken him back so many times when he would disappear and she had believed his pleading words begging her to continue their relationship. Her whole being had been given to Larry and it was he who had given her a sense of hope that she could live a fulfilled life with the love of a man. As a young woman, Grace's dream of a loving relationship had been crushed completely by her destructive marriage. She had foolishly trusted Larry and now he had forsaken her.

It was late evening. Darkness had descended and there was no moon. As Grace looked out of the window, she could see smatterings of images which enfolded her garden – it was November and the bony fingers on the branches of the silhouetted trees seemed to be beckoning to her. The spotlights from the distant houses flickered, reflecting the warmth of the loved ones who inhabited them. Why was she doomed to be alone, she thought. I have tried so hard to be strong but now I can't go on any longer. What is the point of struggling each day when my whole soul has been destroyed? "You have lived your life but because you have been abandoned, there seems no point in continuing," she spoke to herself, as if she were another person. As Grace leaned out of the window; she could feel the cold crisp air gently caressing her face. She stretched further to sense the icy touch of the wind. Looking down onto the garden where she had once stood so happily with Michael all those years ago, Grace wished that she could go back in time to that ecstasy, but she felt herself drowning in darkness as she hauled herself up on to the windowpane. I want to go there and feel the softness of the grass and the happiness I once knew, the voices in her head uttered. She lifted herself further towards the edge of the window, when suddenly two cats screeched and brought her out of the stupefied trance, she was in. She was cold and climbed back into her bedroom and wrapped herself in her duvet as if returning to the womb.

Weeks went by and Grace's mental state began to improve. It was important to her that she should face up to the fact that she would never see her lover again. She would not allow herself to reach that low point under any circumstances. It was terrible to imagine that she could have almost ended her precious life. Determined never to permit her emotions to dominate her actions, Grace started to learn to live her life without a man. It was very difficult and sometimes she would date because she knew that she craved male company and the essence of a physical connection with someone, however brief the outcome. During a visit from an intimate yet platonic male friend who she saw from time to time, Grace received a phone call from Larry, asking if he could see her. This time, however, and to her amazement, she refused his offer, in order to protect herself from any further misery. She was, at last, in control. Strength, had allowed her to say no.

Retirement was something which gave Grace the chance to pursue her many interests. Her parents had died and together with her brother, she inherited a comfortable amount of money which permitted her to feel more secure. This was a new sense of independence where she was able to discover herself and attend to her own needs. A close group of friends helped to encourage her to enjoy her retirement years.

Grace's two grandchildren provided her with such love and affection. She developed a strong relationship with each one. Tara's daughter, Alison, adored her grandmother and she would always bring Grace a gift when she visited. Her visits, accompanied by her mother, were unannounced which somehow seemed to make them more valuable. The closeness that developed made Grace very content as she saw her younger self when she looked at her little granddaughter. Alison had blonde curls and sky-blue eyes, which possessed Grace's sparkle. Even though she was still only young, she loved to help to bake and experimented on her grandmother who politely found everything delicious. It was as if Grace could see the person she might have been as a little girl. On one visit to her, she told Grace that she wanted to be an artist when she got older. Grace responded with a wry smile, loving her granddaughter intensely as she praised her sketches.

It was with great regret that Grace's friend came to tell her that she was moving away. Grace would miss her dreadfully. She understood that their friendship would withstand the distance and although they would be far away from one another, visits would be frequent with telephone calls replacing the long face to face discussions and outings. Through misty tears they spoke their farewell. Grace was now truly alone. Friendship was essential in her life and she knew that her other friends would help her cope with the hardships that she felt certain that she would endure. But Grace felt numb inside. She felt cold and dark and desperately wished for her private life to be nourished by hope. Somehow Grace knew that there was always something different waiting around the corner. For her, there had always been that familiar feeling of having been cursed somehow. She hoped this would now be dissipated. She was trying to be optimistic. Grace had been to the local shops to try and forget the departure of her friend and while driving home, she felt a sadness. Her soulmate was the only one who had really understood her loneliness. She opened the front door and saw her beloved daughter Tara together with her granddaughter Alison busily preparing supper for her. "Come and sit down, Gran Gran. You must be hungry," her granddaughter said in a comforting tone. Grace could ask for no more.

Zoshia 17

Now living alone, Zoshia had time to ponder her life. She felt proud at having brought up three children with successful careers. This had been achieved by a widowed mother with a low income who had struggled and fought to acquire help and support. Having retired, Zoshia felt an emptiness, which could not be filled. She believed that moments of life's happiness were fleeting and the rest of the time was merely remembering. Life had just stolen everything. Her family had been her universe for so long that she felt only a void without them. Even when they visited her, she felt an outsider within their world. It was a realm of youth and she knew that she was no longer relevant. Her youth had been stolen from her in many ways by Adolf Hitler and her early married life had been fraught with trauma.

It was 1992 and old age had crept up on her, strangling her body like a creeping ivy. She had gained weight and felt as if all her bloom of youth had disappeared. When she gazed into the mirror a plethora of freckles greeted her, reflecting all the obstacles in her life which she had been forced to overcome. Would her future be filled with a living sleep which devoured time and ultimately lead to death? Remembering seemed to live in the present, as she contemplated the moments of pleasure that had opened to her like a budding flower, but these moments were contrasted by episodes of difficulty and darkness. Zoshia had known real love and for this she was grateful. She could not decide how much of her life was ruled by positive or negative memories. The feeling of the sun setting on her existence created the clouds which were circling her with a blackening hue.

Zoshia had no idea how to fill her time. She felt no desire to play the piano, as she no longer had the confidence to do so. There was only an empty space which surrounded her each day. The loneliness enveloped her being, as everyone she loved was no longer part of her life. She felt as though everything inside her had died and she was devoid of any hope. For Zoshia, desires were the flowers of those who lived life; they didn't blossom in the realms of decay.

But this outlook changed after Victoria finally confirmed a move back to Liverpool. It was a Wednesday morning, in July 1992. Zoshia was excited once more. She waited with bated breath, as her daughter, Victoria, was driving on the motorway back to her. Her beloved Victoria was returning. Zoshia could never have dreamt that this would happen, and she felt elated, an emotion which she thought she would never feel again. Thinking back to when Victoria was born, Zoshia remembered how Harvey held her in his arms. Their first-born child had made them feel as one body. Neither of them could comprehend the intensity of the love which they felt for this tiny, helpless human being. Victoria was coming home and so Zoshia allowed the excitement to carry her away as she looked in the mirror and smiled. The images that she saw were full of warmth and hope and she felt comforted by the blanket of love that she felt for her daughter.

Zoshia listened as she heard the key being turned to open the door. Victoria had reached the end of her journey and had arrived once more into the womb of her family home. As Zoshia held her first born with a vice-like hug, she felt at this moment that her doubts and fears had subsided and here before her stood her future. Mother and daughter; the suffering she had experienced for so long had resulted in this moment. They were together, creating a closer bond than Zoshia had experienced with anyone in her life. "Come in, babela. You are home."

Although Zoshia adored her daughter, Victoria had been a difficult teenager, which was partly due to Harvey's sickness. There had not been enough time to give her the attention she needed. However, things became very different with an older more mature young woman who had replaced the awkward adolescent. A closeness developed between Zoshia and her daughter, which had never really had time to flourish. She had been so busy working hard all her life to provide a living for her family that she had never made time to just sit and talk. Now that she had retired and was financially comfortable, she was able to communicate to Victoria about her youth and her horrific and courageous experiences during the war; her life with her parents and the struggle of her early married life. Zoshia confided in Victoria about her feelings of isolation living in a foreign country and how she regretted not having made more friends. This seemed to have a cathartic effect upon Zoshia's being. She felt a new affinity with her daughter who seemed to understand her feelings without judging her. Zoshia had at last found someone who empathised with the events that had taken place during her life. She had been searching for this understanding for so long and now she had found it in Victoria, her precious daughter.

The time which they spent alone together was a gift. These were summer moments with flowers of love blooming and enveloping them both. The glorious birth of sunshine represented the brightness of each new-born day. Going out together enabled Zoshia to enjoy the simple pleasures of life once more. Victoria insisted her mother should resume her piano playing and this encouraged Zoshia to feel the delights that she had experienced as a blossoming young woman. When Victoria went out with her friends, Zoshia would refrain from thinking about the past during her acts of musical creativity, as the notes danced sweetly while she played her beloved Chopin.

"A holiday together is what you need," Victoria suggested to Zoshia excitedly. "We will make memories which we can both treasure forever," she added persuasively.

"It's so long since I was in a position to go away, but now… yes, we will," Zoshia replied with a nervous tone in her voice. She was apprehensive but Victoria had given her confidence. So mother and daughter travelled to Fuengirola in Spain and stayed in a hotel which was situated directly on the beachfront overlooking the sea.

As Victoria and her mother sat in a café, which was directly adjacent to the sea, there was a comfortable silence between them as they looked out towards the slow, endless undulating waves that were ebbing towards the shoreline in a rhythmic and pulsating manner. Zoshia loved the ocean; the calm and peace of the swelling of the water seemed to sooth her aching soul. As Zoshia listened to the breakers with her eyes closed, she sensed them creating their own harmonious melody and this seemed like music to her ears; notes that expressed the harmony within her, as she sat peacefully enveloped in the warm sounds of the sea. The gentle breeze distracted her from her trance-like state as she recalled the memories of her parents and her departed husband. This brought no light or joy as she dwelled on the misery of the past. The struggle that Smule and Zara had experienced in the war and the gnawing cancer that destroyed Harvey's life, could not be completely suppressed, as she felt the unnamed sorrow rise within her…" Mum, look at the light from the sun, flickering on the water and the sky seems to be weaved with golden light," Victoria whispered, as if she had just seen a painting in front of her. "Look at the astral-blue horizon that appears to stretch into eternity," she added staring ahead in delight. Zoshia felt at peace now, as her daughter put her arm round her mother affectionately.

On the final evening of their holiday the two women were finishing their desserts in the restaurant. Zoshia was feeling a bit subdued at having to return home. Suddenly, she felt a tap on her shoulder. It was the Maître d'hôtel.

"Madame, we are told that you play Chopin and Beethoven beautifully. We were wondering whether you would play something for us this evening." He winked at Victoria. Zoshia appeared anxious, but bravely stood up and walked nervously towards the piano. Sitting down, she could see the notes of her favourite piece in front of her – not on the piano, but inside her head. Touching the black and white keys familiarly with her fingers, the melodic sound of Beethoven's 'Moonlight Sonata' emanated around the room. The guests and the staff were transfixed. Zoshia played with such passion. This has been a wonderful experience, she thought, as her hands played the piano on their own. Both Zoshia and her daughter would never forget this holiday which brought them together in friendship.

In time, Victoria told her mother that she was in love and wanted to marry. Zoshia was happy for her daughter. Even though this would mean losing her in some ways, she knew that she would always have her first born close by and this took away the pain of her leaving to start her own life. Zoshia loved Harry Cole, too, and she knew that he would take care of Victoria and herself. She prayed and hoped that her precious child, who was marrying late in life, would never have to experience the same hardships that she endured and that her daughter's pathway as a career-minded, modern, independent female, would be a freer and more gratifying one. Zoshia prayed for this as her happiness for her daughter overcame her fear of misfortune.

In her youth, women did not have equality or the same opportunities afforded to Victoria. It had been a man's world, where even educated women struggled to have the satisfaction of pursuing a career and, of course, had to bear the burden of bringing up children at the expense of their own lives. She knew that many women were content with this and relished being a wife and mother. However, it was true also, that there were women born with talents that had often been suppressed completely. Zoshia hoped that times had changed, and the future would hold a different pathway for Victoria whose artistic creativity seemed to have no bounds.

The Final Chapter 18

Grace was painting her latest picture when the invitation was posted through the letter box. She was overwhelmed with joy that her dearest friend was to be married. Despite her cynical attitude towards men and marriage caused by the torture of her experiences, Grace was pleased to be invited. She hoped that life would allow her friend to be happier than she had been; a woman living at the mercy of a male dominated world, with no rights or freedom, just submission. She knew that times had changed, and the tide had turned very much in favour of women's rights and independence but still Grace had lingering doubts about the female role within a marriage. Yet cherishing her friend so much and knowing how utterly in love she was, she would never relay these doubts to her directly. There was an excitement at having to travel by train to a strange city which she had heard of but never visited. As she organised herself, Grace recalled her own excitement as she prepared to marry Peter; she remembered the intense thrill of standing nervously in the registry office with her soon-to-be husband close by her side, believing that this was the culmination of a young, naive woman's search all her young life for true love. This was it, she had thought, as she gazed up at her handsome husband. She had believed at that moment that dreams could be realised.

But in living her dream, the romantic young girl was confronted by the pitiful reality of the severity of daily life. The heatwaves of poverty, a violent marriage, dirty nappies and the fight for survival, were the tramples of the harshness of life itself, which had dealt her many blows. Her sadness lived somehow in the nature of her lost dream.

Grace closed the suitcase just in time to stop a torrent of tears catching the clothes she had just packed so carefully. She took control of her emotions and suppressed those feelings for the time being; she would not travel backwards into her own miserable past, but forwards to her friend's impending wedding. Forwards to all the hopes and dreams that youth offers, and without the suffering and doubts that only come with old age. No, this was her optimistic journey, which she would make for sake of her young friend with whom she had shared so much.

* * *

"You don't have to worry about anything, Mushki. I have organised everything. Just relax," Victoria uttered to her mother, lovingly.

"I know, Babella." Zosha replied, while lovingly admiring her daughter. The two women held hands and kissed each other as only a mother and daughter could. Zoshia wished that her parents and sister were alive to experience the joy that she was feeling. She had not felt quite like this since her own wedding to Harvey in Antwerp. How happy she had been with all her family around her as she started her married life with the man that she loved, not realising what a difficult future she would have to endure. She stopped at once. She must not do this! This bleakness must be stifled. Her daughter had a good career as a teacher and was an independent woman. She knew that Harry would support her in this way and would not stifle her. "Women now have more freedom to live their lives how they want," Zoshia uttered quietly to herself.

Happily, she regained her composure and smiled as she watched her beloved Victoria ticking lists and mulling through replies to invitations. She noticed that her daughter stopped to read one for quite some time. Noticing her eyes becoming filled with tears, Zoshia became concerned. What could possibly make her daughter cry like this? Victoria looked up at her mother and then turned her eyes back to the reply for a moment. Her eyes reread the text and she smiled as she stood up and hugged her mother with such power that Zoshia felt she would break. No words were spoken but the actions of love seemed to matter. Zoshia and Victoria knew that this was real love; love that counted.

* * *

The train journey to another part of the country made Grace, who was travelling alone, feel as though she was leaving herself behind and moving through the motion of the train into someone else's life. She watched the landscape fly past her with visions of her memories flashing before her eyes. She saw her father and mother sternly looking back at her through the windowpane and images of Peter's fierce face rose up slowly from the hard, metal railway tracks. Grace could see her own children running in the meadow, happy and carefree. She imagined Larry looking at her closely from the empty seat opposite her, with his handsome, charming smile. His smile had betrayed her. She had loved him deeply and nearly ended her life because of him, as she remembered the moon which seemed to have left her too on that fateful night – a memory that would haunt her forever. Grace saw Alison smiling at her through the glass window of the train and she gazed up from her drawings with a reassuring look, Grace was propelled back to reality. She was shocked and surprised that during this journey, the past had taken her over completely, leaving no room for the present. Excitement replaced these sojourns into days gone by, as she prepared to arrive at Liverpool's Lime Street Station.

* * *

"Hurry up, Babella or you will be late to collect your friend," Zoshia called to her daughter urgently. She could see that Victoria was very excited.

There was something strange about her enthusiasm as she chattered. "I can't wait for you to meet her, Mushki." Zoshia didn't really understand her daughter's elation but was happy for her. "I'm off to collect her now and will bring her here," Victoria called, as she ran out to the car. Zoshia watched her six-year-old child waving to her as she ran along the path under the pastel, rose covered arch framing the gateway. Her adult daughter turned to wave to her mother, which brought Zoshia's mind back to the present. As Victoria drove off, Zoshia stood in the porch and saw her two young sons playing at being cowboys behind the bushes. She could hear little Victoria's cries as she shouted at the boys for drawing on her beloved doll's head.

Those moments have gone, Zoshia thought to herself. They have been replaced… She saw the German soldiers running across the rooftops and could hear the sound of their jackboots as they marched determinedly past her gate. The children with yellow stars beckoned to her, as they were thrown violently into the van… Oh why did these visions have to plague her at the very moment when she should be happy? She braced herself. Knowing her own real strength, Zoshia closed the front door. Thinking about her daughter's happiness, she went into the kitchen to put the kettle on and set the table. The cake she had made (her mother's recipe) looked very inviting.

* * *

Grace's dear friend was at the station to welcome her. How good it felt to see her again; someone she trusted completely and who she could rely on. The age difference had never mattered in their relationship. Their friendship was real and honest. It was love. "I'm so glad you're here, Grace," Victoria uttered in an excited voice.

"I don't know what to say, except that I wish you every happiness," Grace mumbled sincerely, but with difficulty.

"Come on, my car isn't too far away," her friend said pulling her along and laughing gaily. Victoria knew how difficult it was for dear Grace to make this journey. As they drove to Victoria's family home, Grace became filled with excitement and expectation. She had never seen Victoria look so happy. This abated her earlier feeling of doubt and, as Grace looked at her, she could see someone who had been reborn through finding sincere and honest love.

As they arrived at Zoshia's house, a strange sense of something known, of something shared, enveloped Grace's being. Walking up the path tentatively, she felt an odd familiarity which she could not comprehend. Zoshia peered nervously through the curtains and watched Grace arrive. A peculiar form of consciousness inexplicably pervaded her being. Looking curiously at her daughter's friend she could see…

Zoshia opened the door and the two women just gazed at each other in simple silence. In each other's eyes they saw their own plight, their own grief and their own suffering. They were strangers, yes, but in that moment, they experienced an affinity between them. Instinctively they both moved to each other and embraced. They wept as if they would never stop. Grace and Zoshia clung to each other, bound by the scars they shared, each knowing and recognising the other's pain. In unison, the two women turned to Victoria and looked at her with hope as she stood on the threshold of married life. They then stared back at each other. Their tears had gone.